She saw sparks of devilry in his eyes

"Would you mind if I gave you a congratulatory kiss, Miss Derwent?"

She lifted her face mutely and felt her heart race as Heath rested his lips on her own. They stood like that for a long moment.

Then somehow Sasha seemed to unfreeze her muscles to do the craziest thing. A tiny detached corner of her mind observed the process and immediately flashed bright red warning signals, but she ignored these signals and with a temerity she had never believed she was capable of, brought her hands up to slide them under his jacket.

And then she froze again.

You shouldn't be doing this, Sasha, something deep inside her warned. *You're playing with fire.*

But the fire was well and truly lighted, and the fact that Heath's hands had moved gently on her shoulders didn't put it out....

Perhaps Love

Lindsay Armstrong

Harlequin Books

TORONTO • NEW YORK • LONDON
AMSTERDAM • PARIS • SYDNEY • HAMBURG
STOCKHOLM • ATHENS • TOKYO • MILAN

Original hardcover edition published in 1983
by Mills & Boon Limited

ISBN 0-373-02582-3

Harlequin Romance first edition November 1983

CHAPTER ONE

SASHA Derwent stuck her pen behind one ear and thought for a moment. Then she called out, 'Try the top left dresser drawer! I'm sure I put them in there.'

Or was it the right? she pondered. Oh well, it won't hurt him to look in both.

But she didn't resume work immediately. Instead, she stared out through the french doors, over the paddocks and the river towards the mountains shrouded in a blue haze beyond. It was going to be a beautiful day, she thought with a faint tinge of longing. A day for swimming or riding.

'Or fishing,' she murmured out aloud. 'I bet that's what Dad's planning to do. Or,' she took her glasses off and polished them, 'flying away in a jet to Tahiti!'

She sighed suddenly as she replaced her glasses and wondered why she felt so restless.

'I always knew you couldn't tell your left from your right, Sasha.' It was a muffled, disembodied voice that floated through to her to interrupt her thoughts. 'But I thought by now you might have learnt to distinguish top from bottom. Hell!'

Several thuds accompanied this, and Sasha closed her eyes and laughed silently as she pictured the rickety old dresser, which her employer insisted was an antique, performing its favourite trick and disgorging all its fiddly little drawers to the floor.

She waited, and wasn't disappointed. More clearly audible curses came, followed by an imperative demand. 'Where the devil are you, anyway, Sasha? I also want to talk to you!'

'Coming,' she called back resignedly, and schooled

her face to seriousness.

'Well, you're taking your time about it,' Heath Townsend said into her ear, making her start convulsively.

'Oh! I didn't hear you come in,' she said, half-turning towards him. 'What did you want?'

'You,' the man behind her said promptly. 'Desperately.'

'Oh?' Sasha said mildly. 'Have you cleared it with your mother?'

'As a matter of fact I haven't seen the old Gorgon this morning.'

Heath Townsend removed his well-built frame and famous profile from behind her to lounge against the desk opposite her own in the beautifully appointed study-cum-boudoir that served his equally famous mother as an office.

'Is she up?' he enquired.

'Been and gone,' Sasha said laconically. 'Hours ago,' she added.

'Where to?'

'All over the place,' Sasha said truthfully as she drew a stack of papers towards her and pulled her pen from behind her ear. 'But I could get a message to her if it's important.' She examined the papers, but unseeingly, and wondered what was coming, because with Heath one could never tell.

She wasn't to be disappointed.

'Well, we don't need her approval, then, do we?' he said with a faint grin. 'We could elope.'

Sasha lifted her eyes involuntarily and immediately winced at the full impact of Heath Townsend. All six foot two of his lean, unobtrusively but nevertheless well-muscled frame, topped this morning by an unruly mass of thick, gold-streaked hair and almost navy-blue eyes in a clear, tanned complexion. He was wearing a blue track suit and he glowed with vibrant health and vitality.

Really, she thought with a tiny inward sigh, it just wasn't fair to have so much going for you. It wasn't as if he was precisely good-looking in a conventional, even-featured, male model way. Not if you analysed him feature by feature. But it all added up to a devastating sum of subdued power, glinting humour, almost frightening intelligence and, above all, sheer masculinity. A dynamic combination to which few females were immune as she very well knew.

'Er ... did you say elope?' she said, suddenly realising that the pause was beginning to stretch. She pretended to consider it with her eyebrows raised and her head to one side. 'Well,' she temporised, and then shrugged, 'perhaps another day. I'm really awfully busy.'

'Sweet Sasha,' he murmured. 'Always such a busy little bee.' He straightened up and with a swift movement reached behind her to release the clasp that confined her hair so that the dark auburn strands tumbled down to her shoulders. 'Have you ever slept with anyone, Sasha?' he asked as he arranged the long tresses more to his liking.

She grimaced wryly and and suffered his ministrations patiently, having learnt from long experience that this was the best way to deal with Heath.

'No,' she said after a small silence.

'I thought not,' he remarked, and stood back to study her. 'You have that look.'

'Do I?' she answered with a rueful smile and an odd trip in her heartbeat as she wondered just how she looked to him. Probably the same as I look to myself in the mirror, she thought. Impossibly fair skin, grey eyes and some peculiar thing that keeps me looking like a sixteen year old even although I'm nineteen—almost.

'Yes, you do,' he said, breaking in on her thoughts. He leant over and took her glasses off. 'Why are you wearing these?'

She rubbed her eyes. 'My contact lenses seem to be irritating my eyes, so I thought I'd have a break from them.'

Heath studied her naked eyes thoughtfully. Then he said, 'Well, how about it? Should we take the world by storm and elope? I'm quite in the mood to do something unusual.'

That's strange, she thought, so am I . . .

But she said rather hastily, 'Really, not today, Heath. I . . .'

'Does that mean, not with me?' he interrupted as he carefully replaced her glasses, 'or just that it isn't a good day to elope?'

She said wryly, 'It means, Heath, that I know you're teasing me. Because, I suspect the cupboard fell out all over the floor. Why don't you go and work out some really teasing questions for the Leader of the Opposition, though? You are due to interview him tonight, you know.'

He considered this with his arms folded across his chest and a glint in his eye. 'I know. But do *you* know I've never offered to elope with anyone before, Sasha? And I'm quite deflated by your response.'

'You are not!' she said crossly but with a suspicion of a laugh in her voice. 'And why would you offer to elope with them anyway? You can get it all without having to marry them!'

He grinned wickedly. 'True,' he agreed, and she blinked at the glint of sheer devilry in his eyes. 'On the other hand,' he went on, 'it looks as if you might be my first failure. Is there someone else? To whom do I owe this first taste of defeat?' He narrowed his eyes. 'Don't tell me,' he said swiftly. 'I wondered why I seemed to be falling over Mike Gibson so often these days. Everywhere I turn I'm tripping over our earnest young law student friend. So that's it!'

'It is not!' she snapped, definitely cross this time.

'Anyway, it's none of your business, and I wish you'd go away and leave me alone!'

'Aha,' he said softly, and touched her faintly pink cheek. 'Methinks the lady doth protest too much! So that's the way the wind blows.' He looked at her with the amusement replaced by something more sober. 'I'm not sure if he's the right one for you, though, Sasha.'

'Why not?' she demanded indignantly. 'What's wrong with Mike? Not that I'm ... but anyway,' she added in some confusion, 'I ...'

'There's nothing wrong with Mike per se,' said Heath quite seriously. 'I'm just not sure if he's right for you. He seems to take himself awfully seriously, and sometimes those kind of people can be rather painful in large doses. Also ...' He hesitated.

'What?' she asked curiously.

'Well, very young men like that can be ... not the best teachers sometimes, for very young—for a very young and innocent girl like you. Especially if they're a bit taken up with themselves—the young men, I mean.'

'I'm not that young,' she protested defensively, and added, 'neither is he. He's twenty-two and he's very bright!' She stopped suddenly and wondered why she was rushing to Mike's defence. Was it because Heath had put his finger on something in Mike's personality that had caught her awareness although she wouldn't have been able to express it?

She shrugged. 'Anyway, this is all academic. I wasn't exactly planning to elope with him either. In fact I've only been out alone with him half a dozen times.'

He grinned faintly. 'I see. I wonder how he'd react if he knew you classified him as something academic?'

'I wouldn't know,' she said shortly, 'but because you're thirty-two and he's only twenty-two—well, I think it's unfair to be so critical.'

Heath raised his eyebrows but said nothing, although the laughter was back in his eyes, which annoyed her for some strange reason, so that she said stiffly, 'And besides that, I don't think you, of all people, should be sermonising on ... on that subject.' She finished speaking hurriedly as he raised an impatient hand.

'Now for Pete's sake, don't start lecturing me, Sasha,' he said with the laughter firmly planted in his eyes. 'My mother does enough of that.'

The mention of his mother brought Sasha up with a jerk. 'Yes. Well,' she said a little acidly, 'speaking of your mother, I do have a lot of work to do for her. So if you really wanted to see me about something and not just torment the life out of me, can we get on with it?'

He considered for a moment. 'There was something else,' he said finally. 'Could you—rather, would you—consent to by my companion for dinner tonight?'

Sasha flinched. 'I'd rather not,' she said quietly after a moment.

'Why not?' he queried. 'You've done it before.'

'I know. But you must admit it's a bit of a hassle, and besides, I ... well, I feel a bit silly, if you know what I mean.'

She glanced up at him and bit her lip at his look of bland ignorance, then said in sudden exasperation, 'Yes, you do! You know very well what I mean! Anyway, what's wrong with Veronica?'

'Nothing,' he said idly, referring to his latest mistress. 'Listen, if you're trying to tell me you have nothing to wear—in a roundabout kind of a way—that's a very minor consideration and one of which I've had considerable experience. In fact I could fix that in a tick.' His blue eyes danced with amusement.

She ground her teeth in frustration. 'I'm not trying to tell you anything of the kind! I have a perfectly good dress ...'

'That blue one?' he interrupted. 'The one you wore when we went to the Logie Awards? I don't know,' he said very seriously. 'It made you look like a twelve-year-old trying to be a thirty-year-old. Not quite your style. Besides, you need more delicate colours. Smoky greys, hyacinth, oyster, lilac—black might suit you, actually, in the right dress. It might make your skin look pearly . . .'

'Don't go on,' Sasha said wearily. 'I can't imagine why you're so persistent! A badly dressed virgin can't possibly be what you really want to be seen about with. Surely you can find someone more suitable?'

'Sasha . . .'

'Maybe someone less busy too?' she entreated. 'Your mother would be hopping mad with me!'

'No, she wouldn't,' he said definitely.

'She will, Heath!' Sasha said imploringly. 'Look, I'm terribly fond of your mother, but you know what she's like when things get behind. Why, she'd never let either of us forget it!'

'Not this time, Sasha,' he said smoothly. 'Otherwise she wouldn't have made the suggestion herself last night.'

'*She* suggested it? But I don't understand! Why didn't you say so earlier?' she demanded. 'Why didn't she say anything?' She stared at him bewilderedly.

'She must have forgotten. She doesn't have the best memory in the world for some things, as you should know, of all people.' He shrugged. 'But I can assure you I have her permission to hi-jack her private secretary for the rest of the day.' He turned away and then said over his shoulder. 'Oh, by the way, we'll be leaving a bit earlier than usual.'

'Oh yes. Why?' she asked ominously.

'Because the channel rang me earlier to let me know the chopper is out of action this morning, so we'll have to drive into town. Which gives you—forty-five minutes precisely, to get ready.' He glanced at his watch as he spoke. 'But that should be plenty of time, Sasha,' he added with a grin. 'Just bring yourself. We'll paint the lily when we get to town.'

He strolled out of the room without a backward glance, obviously unaware of how close he came to receiving a blunt object against the head.

'I sometimes wonder why I put up with them!' Sasha muttered to herself. She expelled a long, angry breath and snapped open a drawer.

'Don't be stupid,' she answered herself as she stacked her papers away and shut the drawer forcefully. 'You know very well why!'

She sat back and took her glasses off to rub her eyes. If she was honest, she had to admit she loved every minute of this job, which she had had since she was an impossibly shy seventeen-year-old. That was the year after Heath and his mother had bought this property and horse stud which ran down to the Hawkesbury adjacent to Sasha's own home. The year after Sasha had left school and lost her mother all in a matter of weeks. Stephanie Townsend had been a godsend to both Sasha and her father—an unobtrusive neighbour who had somehow always managed to be there when they'd needed someone. And this had been no mean feat either, because as a successful politician, Heath's mother was an extremely busy woman. But having been widowed herself, Stephanie well knew the special anguish of it.

It had also been the year Sasha had suffered the devastating pangs of an adolescent crush on the not-so-oft-glimpsed Heath. A year of loneliness and introspection on both counts—for her mother and Heath.

But the better she had got to know Heath, who'd treated her like a kid sister, the harder it had been to spend her life dying of unrequited love, and she had finally even managed to transfer most of her unspoken passion to a series of television stars.

If Heath or Stephanie Townsend, or even her father, had ever divined her state of mind then, they had nobly refrained from ever mentioning it. And when Stephanie had, out of the blue, offered Sasha the post of resident private secretary, Sasha had been able to make a most happy transition to a job she loved which had the added bonus of being just across the fence from her beloved father.

Although ... she smiled ruefully and had to admit that on the odd occasion, like this morning, it was a bit like living with a personalised version of one's favourite movie star. Not that Heath was home that much, though. And when he was, he was usually so nice and ordinary, it *was* like having an elder brother.

'Well, almost,' she conceded ruefully, and smiled suddenly. 'But then I guess Heath's a bit special to millions of people really.'

Heath Townsend had first become a name to be reckoned with during the Vietnam war. He had spent six months fighting in the jungles of South-East Asia before being wounded and most honourably discharged from service. But once he had recovered from his wounds he had returned, this time as a journalist, and had fearlessly covered the remainder of the war at great personal risk. And written through every article he had ever presented had been the theme of the utter foolishness and wastefulness of war—particularly that one.

And one way or another he had been covering wars ever since in the Middle East, South America, Iran, Kampuchea, Afghanistan. But now his interests had broadened to general current affairs and home politics, and his television programme was widely acclaimed for its high standard of journalism. As an interviewer he had the knack of seeing all sides, not being biased but being devastatingly acute at the same time, and had been known to drive many a politician, including his mother, to tearing out their hair with his hard-hitting questions and uncanny ability for exposing vague evasions for exactly what they were.

He was also one of the most sought-after bachelors in the state and received sacks of fan-mail from lady admirers of all ages. But, so far, he had married no one, although the list of his affairs was long and much publicised in the gossip columns.

Sasha rubbed her eyes again and thought of Veronica Gardiner.

Veronica was co-producer of his television show as well as having her own weekly spot on it. And Veronica Gardiner was something else again—impossibly sexy-looking on some nights and yet on others managing to look just like the kind of girl no man would mind taking home to meet his mother.

A woman for all seasons, Sasha thought a trifle enviously. But as it had turned out, Veronica hadn't quite made it with Heath's mother, who could on occasions be just as impatient, autocratic and haughty as her son.

'Useless, bloodsucking *leech*!' Sasha had heard Stephanie Townsend remark once.

'But she's so brainy!' Sasha had been moved to reply in surprise. 'I mean, it's like a meeting of two great minds. And it isn't as if she's not good-looking.'

'Two great minds!' Stephanie had snapped with so much viciousness Sasha had blinked. 'My foot!' Her employer had gone on, 'What he needs is someone who'd give him a couple of babies, a bit of cheek and some sane, down-to-earth common sense. I can't see Veronica doing that. She'll probably opt out of having babies altogether for fear she'd ruin her figure.'

Not that his mother had burdened Heath with her feelings on the subject of Veronica. Not that it would have made any difference if she had.

'And that reminds me,' said Sasha as she stood up and finished tidying her desk. 'Just why am I filling in for Veronica tonight? Perhaps . . . of course! She must be out of town. Or something like that.'

But as she sat beside Heath on the long drive to town, all thoughts of Veronica Gardiner had fled from her mind, chased away by a good old-fashioned dose of the sulks. I mean, she thought, he didn't even think of asking me himself! His mother had to suggest it before he bulldozed me into this assignment. But if you try and refuse either of them anything, you only end up appearing incredibly churlish and stubborn. Why do I put up with it?

And the fact that she was travelling in a superbly comfortable, high-powered luxury car that was probably the envy of every other motorist on the road didn't cool her sense of injury. In fact it made her more annoyed than ever, and she compressed her lips into a tight line as Heath guided the car along with unspoken contempt for everyone else on the road and at such a wicked speed that they reached Parramatta in little short of record time.

'Am I going too fast for you?' he asked with a sideways glance at her taut features.

'Not at all,' she replied politely. 'If I'm going to be smashed to pieces, I'm sure it's better not to have time to see it coming.'

'Why don't you unclench your fists, then,' he said lazily. 'Before you stop the circulation completely and your fingers drop off.'

Sasha narrowed her eyes and stared straight ahead, her mouth set anew in a grim, angry line.

Heath laughed at her quietly. 'I've never seen you so angry before, Blossom,' he said softly.

That did it, she found. Blossom was her father's pet name for her, and he'd used it for as long as she could remember. As did most other people who knew her. But now at nearly nineteen it sounded slightly incongruous even on her father's lips, she sometimes thought, let alone Heath's, and whenever he used it teasingly, she couldn't help thinking of a gurgling baby.

And without giving herself time to think further, she rounded on him and said furiously, '*Don't* call me that! And yes, I am angry. In fact I'm furious, and I think you're one of the most self-opinionated men I've met! I didn't enjoy being told that dress didn't suit me. I didn't enjoy your comments on how young and innocent I am, as if I'm some silly schoolgirl still, and I didn't like being yanked off at a moment's notice. so I'm not only angry, I'm well and truly piqued. Added to this,' she went on bitterly, 'I'm not exactly jumping for joy at the prospect of this evening, because everyone knows I'm your mother's secretary and I'm only filling in. But what's worse, I'm sure it doesn't stop them from speculating whether little Sasha Derwent isn't secretly hopelessly in love with you like every other female seems to be. In fact . . .' She trailed off suddenly and unclenched her fists.

'Go on,' he said.

She shrugged. 'In fact I feel a whole lot better,' she confessed with some surprise, and couldn't help smiling at Heath's bewildered expression.

He blinked deliberately. 'Say that again, Sasha? You lost me somewhere along the line.'

'Never mind,' she said lightly.

'But I do mind! I had no idea I was subjecting you to these tortures. And I'm sorry for being so critical . . .'

'It doesn't matter,' she interrupted. 'As a matter of fact I threw it out,' she added grudgingly.

He frowned. 'The blue dress?'

'Uh-huh. I took a pathological dislike to it this morning.' She glanced at him and smiled again at his look of perplexity.

'Does this mean you're coming or not?' he asked quizzically at last.

'Of course. Now I've had my say I'm perfectly resigned to it. But it's going to cost you a dress,' she said easily.

He grimaced wryly and quirked an eyebrow at her. 'All right,' he agreed. 'On one condition—that I choose the dress?' He gave her a lilting smile.

'Sure!' she said unwisely, quite carried away by the sensation of having had her say.

They drove the last few miles in a companionable silence.

Sasha didn't feel quite so companionable, however, at roughly eight-thirty that evening when she was in the dress. *The* dress.

She stared at herself in the mirror of the bedroom that was normally reserved for her use in the elegant harbourside flat that Heath and his mother shared when they were in Sydney. Sasha often stayed at the flat with Stephanie and kept a small selection of clothes there for the occasional rush trips to town, such as this one, that she made with Stephanie.

It was a superb dress. She couldn't deny it. The smoky, bluey-grey colour reminded her of a thundercloud and its silky textured lines clung to her figure as if it had been made for her. It was the design that bothered her. The bodice was sleeveless with the front and the back gathered into a tiny Peter-Pan collar, thus exposing most of her shoulders and slashed beneath the arms to the waist. In some ways, she noticed as she turned this way and that, it looked surprisingly demure, but in others, when she lifted her arms and the soft, pearly flesh of her sides was exposed, it was cunningly revealing.

'Why did I let myself get talked into letting him choose it?' she muttered to herself. 'Why didn't I at least look at it before this?'

Because you didn't have time, Sasha, she reminded herself. What with getting Heath ready for his show and then being lured into going to watch it recorded, you just didn't have time.

She shrugged impatiently and yanked her wardrobe door open, but as she very well knew, there was nothing in it that could be worn tonight.

I should have known! she thought. I should have known when I asked him about it this afternoon and all he would say was that he'd taken care of it. I should have known...

'Heath!' she called imperatively as she opened the bedroom door and stalked out. 'Heath!'

'At your service, ma'am ... oh!' He emerged from his bedroom at the same time and they all but collided in the passageway.

'Well now,' he said as he put out a hand to steady her.

'*Well* now,' she repeated steadily as his eyes flicked over her. 'I conceded that the blue dress might not have been me, but this isn't either!'

'But it's more than you, Sasha!' he told her as he linked his fingers round her wrist. 'The colour suits you and it fits ...'

'What there is of it,' she interrupted tartly. 'Anyway, I haven't the right kind of bra to wear with it. If there is a right kind. Oh!' She stamped her foot and coloured suddenly as his eyes came to rest on her bosom. She pulled her wrist free of his grasp and brought her arms up to fold them angrily across her chest.

'It's not the kind of dress you wear a bra with, Sasha,' he said gravely but with a wry quirk to his lips. 'And despite what they might have told you at that very select private school you attended, Blossom, it's no crime not to wear a bra. A lot of women do it, a lot of very respectable ones too.'

'Well, they shouldn't,' she said through her teeth then bit her lip angrily as he dissolved into silent laughter. 'I despise you, Heath Townsend,' she said in a low fierce voice.

He raised his eyebrows quizzically, his eyes still alive with silent laughter which incensed her so much that she raised one hand unthinkingly to slap him, but this made him look more amused as with a deceptive languor he caught her arm mid-air and pinioned it to her side.

'What you need is a drink, Sasha,' he said gravely as she turned scarlet with rage and mortification. 'Come,' he added, and propelled her into the lounge and sat her down in a silk upholstered armchair.

He poured her a sherry and one for himself. 'Now,' he said, drawing up a chair opposite her, 'let's examine this clinically, shall we? This dress is perfect for you. The colour highlights your pale, perfect skin, and it makes your hair a true, deep auburn. It also matches your eyes almost exactly—I never realised what beautiful eyes you have, Sasha,' he added seriously.

'I ... well, thank you,' she said stiffly. 'It's just that ...' She gestured helplessly.

'You've never worn such a sophisticated dress before?' said Heath acutely. 'But that's where you're wrong. It has a touch of sophistication and a touch of almost ... primness,' he reached and fingered the Peter-Pan collar as he spoke, 'which is very proper and becoming for someone your age. And it's not as if it reveals your breasts at all only ... well, much less of you than one would see in a bikini. You know, Sasha,' he added thoughtfully, 'I think you spend far too much time in the company of old fogies.'

She couldn't help smiling faintly at this. 'Your mother would hate you for saying that,' she murmured.

'Do you think so? I think she'd probably agree if she ever took the time to think about it,' he said humorously.

They laughed quietly together at that, then Sasha drained her glass and set it down carefully. 'Well, if you're sure it looks all right,' she said uncertainly.

'I'm quite sure. You look very attractive, young and

fresh and lovely, and I can guarantee no one will leap on you and try to rape you because you aren't wearing a bra.'

She lifted her eyebrows. 'That sounds like a double-edged compliment,' she said wryly. 'But I didn't think they would anyway.'

'Well, what did you think as a matter of interest?' Heath queried as he refilled her glass.

Sasha flushed, but managed to say evenly, 'I'm not quite as old-fashioned as you imagine, Heath.' She pondered for a moment as she watched the amber liquid in her glass and then shrugged and grinned up at him. 'I only said what I did about bras because you made me cross. But I suppose I'm sort of at the crossroads—about clothes. I really feel that I want to spread my wings and try out some daring fashions, but since I was obviously unsuccessful with the blue dress, I couldn't help wondering if *this* dress might not have the same effect. You know, make me look as if I was trying to be a mature woman of the world when I'm really only a mixed-up kid most of the time.'

He stared down at her for a long moment. Then he said quietly, 'I don't think you're a mixed-up kid at all. Just one of the nicest ones I know. And all women agonise over their clothes.' His lips twitched faintly. 'You'd be surprised! But whatever you wore, Sasha, no one could mistake you for anything but a surprisingly sane, thoroughly nice, well-brought-up . . .'

'Virgin,' she finished for him, and grimaced. 'Thank you, you've set my mind utterly to rest.' She rose and walked to the door, but turned at the last moment and added with a rueful grin, 'And thank you for not adding that I'm about as exciting as homemade apple pie and cream—so far as men go, I mean. I won't be long.'

She didn't see the slight frown that came to his eyes as she left the room.

The dinner party came as something of a surprise to Sasha. It was held in a private function room in one of Sydney's best hotels and wasn't the large gathering she expected. In fact it was a celebration of the second complete year of Heath's television programme and as far as she could see, in a rather shortsighted way since she'd elected not to wear her glasses, she was one of the very few people present not involved in the making of the programme.

This seemed to surprise a few other people, she noted.

But one of the bigger surprises of the evening didn't come until after they were all seated at the large horseshoe-shaped table. It was then that the ornate double doors of the room opened with a flourish and Veronica Gardiner stood there on the arm of a strange man. And the whole gathering sat up and did a discreet double-take.

Sasha felt Heath tense beside her and she looked up at him bewilderedly. But it was George Smythe, the programme's director, a genial-looking man with a chubby face but a cold, sharp wit, who answered the unspoken question in Sasha's eyes.

He said from his seat opposite her, 'I knew it! Our co-producer, despite what she said, couldn't resist this little bunfight, could she? And doesn't she ever love making an entrance! I really don't know how you put up with her for so long, Heath. Professionally yes, but privately . . .' He shrugged and let his sotto voce words hang in the air, quite unperturbed at the smouldering look Heath cast him.

It wasn't far from the double doors to the head of the table, but it took Veronica all of five minutes as she stopped at each person in turn and introduced her companion to everyone. And as she moved with that peculiar sinuous walk that was almost her trademark, her golden dress glittered in the candlelight beneath her magnificent, straw-fair hair, and Heath's eyes took on a strange glitter of their own.

Sasha swallowed and moved uncomfortably in her chair as waiters fluttered about inserting two extra chairs among the diners almost exactly opposite Heath and herself. She discovered her palms were moist with tension as Veronica and her escort came inexorably closer, and she wished fervently that she had trusted her first instincts which had told her to have nothing to do with this party. I was right, she thought numbly. At least, I had some sort of premonition. They must have quarrelled . . .

Then Veronica and the tall dark man with her were standing directly in front of them and Veronica's strange hazel eyes were clashing with Heath's as she said huskily, 'Sorry we're late, darling. As you know, I wasn't going to come, but then I thought, why not? Have you met Brent Havelock? Brent, this is Heath Townsend and George Smythe, and . . .' She glanced at Sasha as if seeing her for the first time, then her beautiful eyes narrowed fleetingly and a slow smile started at the corners of her elegantly chiselled lips. 'Oh dear,' she said lightly, and cast Heath a look of sparkling impudence. 'Dear me,' she murmured, and turned to her escort. 'Brent, this is Sasha Derwent. She's a perfect little pet, besides being Heath's mother's secretary.' She turned back to Sasha. 'How are you, poppet? I must say Heath's surprised me. I quite expected some wildly exotic, gorgeous creature who'd outshine me and put me very firmly in my place. But it's only you, darling. Although you're growing up, Sasha! The last time I saw you, you still had those braces on your teeth. I hope Heath's paying you overtime, darling,' she added playfully.

Sasha sat numb and frozen as the entire room fell silent beneath the strange resonance of Veronica's husky voice.

CHAPTER TWO

IT was an abrupt movement beside her that brought Sasha to life. Heath's hand had shot forward to curl around the stem of his champagne glass and although she was never quite sure how she knew it, his intentions flashed through her mind like a neon light and she moved as swiftly as he had to put a strongly restraining hand over his to stop him from dashing the contents of his glass in Veronica's face.

'How are you, Veronica?' she said at the same time in a voice that surprised her because it was so calm and steady. 'I haven't seen you for ages. Oh!' She looked round and at the same time exerted more pressure on Heath's hand, which had moved convulsively beneath hers. 'You're just in time for the first course,' she remarked brightly as a waiter placed a prawn cocktail before her. 'Do sit down. And you, Brent—may I call you Brent?'

And almost as if at an invisible cue everyone began talking rather feverishly, and after a small hesitation Veronica drew out her chair.

George flashed Sasha an acute, admiring glance as her hand slackened and finally left Heath's in as unobtrusive a gesture as she could make it.

But Heath stared down at the prawn cocktail that had been set before him with a muscle jerking in his jaw and such a blank expression that Sasha trembled anew as she visualised the tiny prawns in pink sauce slipping and sliding down Veronica's décolletage, and she sent George a glance of entreaty. But it didn't happen, because Heath visibly changed gear then and even began to smile.

23

'Brent Havelock,' he said to the prawn cocktail. He raised his devastating dark blue gaze slowly. 'It's good to see you,' he said finally, and before Sasha's bewildered gaze the two men shook hands across the table.

'Heath,' said Brent Havelock, his ruggedly handsome, tanned face set in lines of constraint. 'I didn't know,' he said quietly. 'I've been away for so long.'

'Sure,' said Heath. 'It's good to see you back. How are you?'

Sasha felt her chest muscles relax as Brent sat down. Then she caught sight of Veronica's expression which was, to put it mildly, venomous. But in an instant, as Veronica became aware of Sasha's glance, the venom was wiped off her lovely countenance and Sasha relaxed all over again and drank half a glass of champagne before she had realised what she had done.

A swift, sideways peep at George's face, which registered a comical 'phew' of relief, caused her to drink the other half in celebration, and it wasn't for another ten minutes at least that the feeling of elation that had engulfed her at successfully defusing an explosive situation began to wane.

Why do I feel so deflated now? she asked herself as she sipped her second glass of champagne. She looked around the table. Heath was obviously restored to normal and so was Veronica. Even Brent had lost that curious look of discomfort and was conversing quite normally. If you could call the level of conversation that was being bantered around normal.

'. . . but if you take an out-and-out socialist and suddenly endow him with a substantial inheritance nine times out of ten what do you end up with? A rabid capitalist!' One earnest, bespectacled man was saying passionately.

Sasha closed her eyes and thought, I'm bored! I'm bored with all this theoretical talk where everything that has a name is pounded to death and back again. And again and again.

She turned away, but found that on the other side of her an incredibly bitchy intra-industry gossip session was raging, so she turned wearily back to her filet mignon and thought gloomily, it must be me. But don't any of them have cats or dogs or horses? Or children? Or even gardens or pot plants? Or do they spend their whole life solving these problems?

She pushed her plate away decisively and looked around rather hopelessly for a powder room.

'. . . Sasha?' she heard George say.

'What was that?' she queried vaguely, her eyes still scanning dark corners for a sign of a petticoated lady or a parasol.

'I said,' George remarked patiently, 'don't you agree?'

Sasha sighed and brought her eyes back to rest on George. 'I'm sorry, I didn't hear what you were saying,' she admitted.

Veronica said with an indulgent little smile, 'I think we might be going a bit too deep for Sasha.'

'On the contrary,' Sasha heard herself say swiftly as a tiny collective gasp went round the table, 'I don't think you go deep enough. You were discussing poverty just now, weren't you? As if it was some faintly distressing disease that you were inoculated against. And you spoke of interest rates and unemployment and inflation and how the government should do this or do that, but did you ever think of actually coming to grips with it yourself? Instead of all this talk and suggestion about what other people should do? In fact, do you ever do anything but sit around and look beautiful and expound these high-flown theories?'

'I suppose you do?' Veronica said lazily into the sudden silence.

Sasha looked briefly uncomfortable, and it was Heath who answered for her.

'As matter of fact she does,' he said, looking steadily at Veronica. 'She works in a Salvation Army orphanage whenever she has some free time.'

Veronica laughed—a cold tinkling little laugh. 'Next thing you'll be converted, pet! Do you play a tambourine?'

'No,' said Sasha evenly before Heath could intervene. 'But can I tell you something, Veronica? Do you remember that telethon you took part in to raise money for that spastic children's home? The one where you exposed yourself so gorgeously and almost indecently on the front lawn in an evening gown? Well, I saw some of those children watching you as if you were a . . . fairy queen. But did you go near any of them? No. And I heard what you said as soon as all the photography was over. You said, for Pete's sake get me out of here, someone. You managed to turn a charitable drive to raise funds into an advertising session for Veronica Gardiner. Now I might not be as bright as you, Veronica,' she went on contemptuously, 'but it honestly seems to me that the world survives on example, not talk. So you may philosophise as much as you like, but so far as I'm concerned, you don't have a clue what life is really all about.'

There was a horrid little silence, during which Sasha was the object of all eyes, and if looks could have killed, Veronica's look would have done just that. But what she would have said no one ever knew, because at that moment two waiters entered bearing aloft a huge white birthday cake with two large candles and dozens of sparklers.

'How dare you, Sasha!' Veronica snapped angrily. 'You're nothing but a jumped-up little schoolgirl anyway,' she added contemptuously.

Sasha sat down and then half rose again. 'Perhaps I'd better go,' she mumbled uncomfortably.

'I think we'll both go,' said Heath, and she looked at him fearfully.

'I can get a t-taxi,' she stammered.

'Not at all, my dear Sasha,' he said, and yanked her unceremoniously to her feet. 'We'll both go in style. And don't you dare burst into tears,' he muttered warningly out of the side of his mouth.

'Why should I do that?' she whispered as she was forcibly extricated from the table, but she was horrified to see as she glanced around that most people were looking at her as if she was Attila the Hun personified.

'Because then they'll think you've had too much to drink,' he said very quietly. 'Brent,' he added in a normal voice, 'come and see me soon. Goodnight, all! Enjoy the rest of the party,' he called over his shoulder, and swept her from the room.

'My purse!' Sasha panted as the double doors closed behind them. 'I left it there!'

'Don't worry about it,' he said briskly. 'I'll buy you another one.'

'But it was my mother's!' she protested.

He stopped abruptly and then leant his shoulders back against the passage wall and started to laugh silently.

'What's so funny?' she asked crossly.

'You,' he said, straightening up at last. 'Blossom, I've got no intention of going back in there and I don't think you'd enjoy it either. But I promise you, I'll make sure you get it back tomorrow.' He looked at her consideringly but with a faint lingering grin. Then he held out his arm to her and said gravely, 'Come, Napoleon. I believe he was on the small side, but he too packed a powerful punch.'

She looked at him doubtfully. 'Where are we going?'

'To talk.'

The spot he chose to talk was back at the flat.

Even the weather's conspired against us, Sasha

thought miserably as she stood in the middle of the
elegant lounge. I'm sure he was going to take me to some
romantic moonlit spot on the harbour, but when it
started to thunder and rain . . . She caught her thoughts
with a tinge of incredulity. You've gone crazy, Sasha,
she chided herself. And don't bet that he's not deeply
angry either, because with Heath you can never tell.

He came into the room behind her and tossed his car
keys on to the table. 'A drink?' he said casually as he
crossed to the cedar cocktail cabinet.

She twisted her fingers together. 'No. No thank you.'

'Coffee, then,' he said. 'Mrs Morris left some
percolating, I see.'

She nodded, unable to bring herself to meet his eyes.
They had hardly talked on the way home. She would
have liked to attribute this to the fact that he had had
to concentrate on his driving in the heavy downpour.
But there was a tautness about him she could feel.

She sighed inaudibly and sank down into a chair. He
brought her cup of coffee over and placed it beside her.

'I'm sorry!' she burst out, suddenly unable to
suppress her agitation any longer. 'I'm truly sorry. I
was unforgivable.'

'Were you?' he queried standing straight and tall
beside her chair so that she had to tilt her head back to
look up at him.

'Yes, I was,' she said disconsolately. She winced as she
recalled some of the things she'd said. 'I was so pompous,
and I must have sounded unbelievably self- righteous. If
I'd been listening, I'd have labelled myself a real prig.'

She waited tensely for his reply, but none came. He
simply stared down at her musingly.

She took a deep breath. 'I also had more to drink
than usual,' she said gruffly.

'And were feeling more than a little humiliated at the
hands of our dear Veronica,' he said evenly. 'Not to
mention my own unfortunate remarks earlier.'

She shrugged. 'That too. I don't mean what you said. I got over that hours ago. Besides, you did offer to elope with me,' she said with a glimmer of a smile. 'But Veronica ... I guess she did spur me on. Although I shouldn't have reacted like that. I mean, I know why she did it. She was trying to warn me off. Perhaps in the heat of the moment she just didn't realise I'm no threat to her as far as you're concerned.' She finished uncertainly as a sudden look of pain and bitterness crossed his face.

Then it was gone and he removed her coffee cup from her fingers and drew her to her feet so that they were standing only inches apart.

'Sasha,' he said quietly, 'you sounded as if you really meant all those things you said. And knowing you, I'm sure you did. Don't apologise, because you were magnificent.'

Her mouth dropped open as her eyes widened, causing him to smile wryly, and his hands came up to cup her shoulders. 'Do you know,' he said gently, 'I've been trying to think of a suitable way to salute your ... coming of age. Would you mind if I gave you a congratulatory kiss, Miss Derwent?' he said gravely.

Sasha shut her mouth with a click.

'Does that mean yes or no?' he asked with a smile tugging at the corners of his lips.

She cleared her throat and reached up automatically for her glasses, but of course they weren't there. 'Yes,' she said in a slightly cracked voice. 'Provided you're not just feeling sorry for me.'

He grinned and the tiny sparks of devilry in his eyes took her breath away. 'I don't think I'll ever feel sorry for you again, Napoleon,' he said, but instead of angering her his words seemed to caress her mind almost.

And she lifted her face mutely and felt her heart race

as he rested his lips on her own. They stood like that for a long moment.

Then somehow Sasha seemed to unfreeze her paralysed muscles and do the craziest thing. A tiny detached corner of her mind observed the process and immediately flashed bright red warning signals, but maybe because it had been a crazy day all round, she ignored these signals and with a temerity she had never believed she was capable of, brought her hands up to slide them under his jacket.

And then she froze again.

You shouldn't be doing this, Sasha, something deep inside her warned. You're playing with fire.

But the fire was well and truly lit, she found, and the fact that Heath's hands had, possibly out of sheer surprise, moved gently on her shoulders, didn't help put it out.

She trembled and found that the elegant room swirled before her eyes. So she closed them and whispered, 'Could you kiss me properly, please?'

She felt his taut diaphragm move beneath her hands and knew immediately that he was laughing at her. Well, I've been laughed at once too often today, she thought fiercely. Let him laugh at this!

She moved her hands downwards about his waist and slowly round and then up his back across the thin silk of his shirt. She did it lingeringly feeling every rippling muscle and the ridge of his scars, and at the same time she moved into his arms.

'I would really like to be kissed,' she murmured. 'Not *saluted*. After all, I shall be nineteen in a few weeks,' she added rebelliously as he didn't stir.

'I know that,' he said very quietly against the corner of her mouth. 'But it's . . .' He hesitated.

'Is it such a penance?' she whispered back.

He didn't answer, yet she felt his hands tighten and he moved his head. But it wasn't her lips he sought, only the slender column of her neck to trail a line of butterfly kisses down it.

'Kiss me, please, Heath,' she whispered deep in her throat. 'Don't torment me like this.'

But despite her plea, she found she was still unwittingly wary and untutored as his lips at last found her own.

'Relax,' he murmured. 'Let me do the work until you catch on.'

Sasha did as she was bid, and soon she was kissing him back as if she had been born knowing how to do it.

'Oh, Heath,' she stammered when she felt that if he let her go, she would fall, 'don't stop, please!'

He laughed silently. 'You're a fast learner, Sasha. Come.'

'Where?' she asked, and opened her eyes as he picked her up and moved a few short steps to a wide settee.

'Just here,' he said reassuringly, and sat her down in his lap. He reached out and flicked off the lone lamp that illuminated the room.

She stared across at the wide windows, uncurtained to capture the fabulous view. A bright pale moon rode high above the silver edged clouds.

'The storm's gone,' she said wonderingly as she turned to snuggle closer to him.

'Yes,' he said. 'Sasha, I think we should stop and examine this before we get in too far.' His voice was deep and had a quality to it she couldn't identify.

'What's to examine?' she asked after a moment with a catch in her voice, and dropped her hand which had been tenderly exploring the strong lines of his throat.

Heath didn't speak for a long moment, and she suddenly felt as if she wanted to curl up and die of embarrassment and humiliation.

She sat up and said in a tight little voice, 'Of course. I'm afraid I got a bit carried away.' She tried to laugh lightly, but it didn't come off. So she attempted to scramble up off his lap, but he held her back until she lay in his arms panting with frustration and a deeper misery she didn't dare name.

'Lie still,' he said quietly, and dropped a chaste kiss on her forehead.

She felt the tears well. 'I'm . . . I don't know what to say,' she murmured disjointedly. She tried to smile up at him in the reflected moonlight. 'But I'll be back to normal by tomorrow, I promise,' she added. 'No more fatuous speeches. No more . . .' Her voice trailed off.

'Sasha,' he said, his eyes resting on her trembling lips, 'don't reproach yourself, sweetheart. It's all very natural to feel this way sometimes. But at the same time it's a very big step for you, and one that you might never have contemplated making if you hadn't had a rather traumatic day.'

'But not for you?' she queried huskily, then bit her lip. 'I mean . . .'

'I know what you mean,' he interrupted, and smoothed her hair from her forehead. 'It's not that, but it's not exactly the first time for me.'

Sasha moved in his arms and couldn't deny she revelled in the feel of it. 'Do you want me to be honest?' she asked shyly, then grimaced. 'Don't answer that. I'm sure you don't. I've been quite honest enough for one night.'

'Yes, I do,' he said seriously.

'I . . . no, I can't,' she conceded abruptly, suddenly equally serious. 'So you'd better let me go to bed.' And found that the mere mention of the word left her feeling hot and cold.

'Tell me,' said Heath intently and without the slightest sign of effort, easily resisted all her attempts to leave his lap.

'How can I?' she said brokenly at last. 'I've already made *such* a fool of myself.'

'Not with me you haven't. You could never do that,'

Sasha. Listen, when two people get this close there's only one way to be, and that's totally honest. If I didn't believe that I wouldn't have stopped just now.'

'And I think you're also just a little amused,' she said tearfully.

It was a curious expression that crossed his face then in the pale moonlight. A mixture of pain and weariness, she thought. And she believed him despite herself when he said very quietly, 'I was never more serious in my life, Blossom.'

'All right!' she said desperately. 'What can I say? From the first moment I laid eyes on you I thought—I mean, I wondered . . . Oh, how can I say it!' she finished miserably.

'I know that,' he said very quietly, and stilled her sudden urgent movement with his hands. 'And that's another thing that's perfectly natural. It happens all the time when you're at that age. I can remember when I was sixteen I fell violently in love, so I thought, and I told myself it was the real thing. But it wasn't,' he said gently.

Oh no! she thought, he knew. All the time he knew! And she wrenched herself out of his arms and with a few backward, stumbling steps and aided by a large footrest that stopped her from falling, she moved out of his reach.

Heath stood up in one swift, fluid movement. 'Sasha,' he said sombrely.

She stared up at him, stricken. Then she whispered, 'Please, just let me go now.' And she turned towards the doorway with jerky, unco-ordinated movements and tripped over a large Chinese vase.

Oh no! she thought despairingly. Thank heavens for the carpet. And why aren't I wearing my glasses!

She restored the vase and stumbled for the doorway. But just as she reached it a hand fell on her shoulder.

'Sasha.'

'G-goodnight,' she said breathlessly without turning.

'No, it's not goodnight.' The overhead light flicked on and she found she was trapped like some moth on a curtain by the unexpected radiance and his hand on her shoulder, turning her towards him.

'Please, Heath,' she whispered, 'don't do this to me.'

'But I must,' he said as he turned her fully around and put a hand beneath her chin. 'Look at me, Sasha,' he said authoritatively.

'I *can't*!'

'Yes, you can. You must,' he added compellingly as he studied her downcast lids, 'because we've been such good friends up until now. And because I admire you so much.'

Her eyelashes swept upwards involuntarily then. 'But not enough to ... to want to love me?' she whispered.

His fingers moved beneath her chin. 'I do love you,' he said. 'There's so much I love about you. I love you when you're ... when you haven't got your glasses or your lenses on and you trip over things. I love you when you make speeches and out of your heart, hit on the problem that's been plaguing me for ages. I love the way you handle my mother—and me, for that matter.'

Sasha stared up into the dark blue of his eyes and felt her heart beat like a tom-tom. 'You said,' her voice was shaky, 'this morning you said I'd be better off with an older man to teach me about ... about ...'

'Sasha,' he said, looking unbelievably grim, 'I don't, in any one day of my life, think I've said more things that I regret having said. Or done. But for what it's worth, what I meant was, I don't think Mike Gibson loves *you*, so much as he loves himself, and that you would just be an ... addition to his crown of self-admiration. And you rate far more than that, which a more mature, not necessarily older person would see. But *I'm* not that person.'

'I see,' she said after a long silence, and felt a tear tremble on her lashes.

'Do you?' he said with infinite patience as he smudged the tear from her cheek. 'Do you really know what I am? I honestly believe I'm the kind of man who perhaps won't ever be ready to be tied down to one woman. I have a restlessness in my soul that I can't still. And a sort of cynicism in my heart about so many things, women particularly, that I hate but I can't shake. That's the true me, Sasha.'

She stared up at him and caught her breath at the sudden longing that flooded her. A longing that grew almost unbearable as she searched every inch of his face and saw, as if it was written plainly, the disillusionment, the pain and the soul-weariness that was normally so effectively masked. A desperate longing to be able to smooth it away somehow. And her heart tightened as she realised she would dearly love to be able run Veronica through with a sharp knife for contributing to it all.

She swallowed and moistened her lips. 'I do understand, Heath,' she said barely audibly. 'I'm sorry I . . .'

'Don't!' he said violently and placed his fingers on her lips. 'You don't have to apologise to me. If anything, it should be the other way around. Blossom,' he hesitated and then drew her into his arms and said into her hair, 'you will meet the right man some day and then you'll be able to look back at this and laugh.' He held her tighter as a tremor shook her body. 'Just give it time,' he said quietly. 'Don't rush into anything—you've got so much time on your side. And then when you do find someone who loves you as much as you love him, that will be the very best way to be taught *and* to teach. Believe me.' He hugged her close and then stood her out at arm's length. 'I know that sounds rather like—do as I say, not as I do, coming from me,' he said with a faint grin as he tucked a strand of her hair behind her ear, 'but for you, I believe it.'

Sasha closed her eyes and called on every ounce of

will-power she possessed. 'Well, if I'm not allowed to apologise can I just say thank you?' she asked, her voice husky and uneven, and she prayed as she spoke that she would have the strength to open her eyes and not cry.

Afterwards, she never knew how she managed it, but she did—even to smile slightly before she turned at the look of compassion in his eyes and walked to her bedroom. Where the control she had achieved slipped drastically so that she flung herself on to her bed and cried herself to sleep.

CHAPTER THREE

IT was a beautiful morning that greeted Sasha's tired, reddened eyes when she finally woke. All traces of last night's storm had disappeared leaving the world clean and fragrant. And the sun glittered and reflected on the harbour waters so that they sparkled and danced beneath a blue, blue sky and the sails of the Opera House looked breathtakingly white and pure in the bright morning light.

Which is more than I can say for myself, Sasha thought as she inspected herself in the mirror. I certainly don't sparkle and I feel as if I've been under a steamroller. They say love agrees with you, adds a bloom, but they must not mean unrequited love.

She flinched and bit her lip, staring at her reflection minutely as if it would yield some secret she couldn't grasp. Is it really love? she wondered. Or *is* it just an adolescent crush as he thinks? But if that's so, why do I have this terrible feeling as if something's been torn out of me?

Perhaps, an inner voice prompted, because until last night, when you gave yourself away like some naïve schoolgirl, you had a subconscious idea that one day, by some miracle, it wouldn't be unrequited love? But now you know it can never be.

'Perhaps you're right, Sasha,' she told her reflection in the glass. 'And if I'd never said anything or done anything,' she shivered suddenly as she remembered how she had begged Heath to kiss her, 'perhaps you might have found that this feeling just faded away like an old daydream as time went by.'

But now, instead, she mused, I shall be horribly

embarrassed whenever I think of Heath, let alone see him, despite what he said to me last night. How could I not, whether it's love or whatever? she asked herself.

She shivered again as this thought brought her slap bang up against the fact that she was going to have to do just that very shortly. See Heath and drive home with him and go on seeing him from time to time.

Despite her misgivings, however, as she sat across the breakfast table from him, she thought she was managing it all very well. True, she was more subdued than usual, she acknowledged, and she had no doubt that he understood why. And indeed he was rather that way himself. But that he wasn't going to accept this state of affairs didn't occur to her until just after their hands had brushed accidentally over the marmalade and she had coloured faintly and unknowingly looked a picture of misery.

'Hell,' he said abruptly. 'This is no good.' And as she looked at him warily he reached for the phone and dialled his mother's number.

But if she had started out looking at him warily, by the time he had finished speaking into the phone and then calmly replaced it on his parent's agonised squawks, Sasha's eyes were wide and incredulous.

'What did you do that for, Heath?' she stammered.

'Several reasons,' he said with a grimace. 'One, it's going to be a beautiful weekend, two, she works you like a slave anyway and one weekend without you might just make her realise it, three, you look as if you need a good tonic. And four, I can't bear the thought of us parting like this, Sasha, with you looking so guilty and unhappy and uncomfortable. Because I really do treasure your friendship, and this just might be the way to get it back. Otherwise I'll be plagued by the thought that you're going to spend the rest of your life avoiding me.'

His words were light enough, but he watched her

keenly as he spoke and didn't miss the chord his words struck. 'I thought so,' he said wryly. 'But that's not really the Sasha I know. She's made of tougher stuff, and if you don't believe me go and ask a certain mob of people who happened to cross swords with her last night.'

She couldn't help laughing a little then. 'Oh, Heath,' she said, 'don't remind me! But what will we do?' she asked bewilderedly.

'Sasha,' he said solidly, 'we'll do what we both probably haven't had time to do for years. I know I haven't anyway. We'll enjoy this fair city of Sydney as it's crying out to be enjoyed on days like these. We'll take a hydrofoil across the harbour to Manly for a swim. Then we'll come back in a more stately manner on the ferry to Rose Bay and have an enormous seafood lunch on the deck in the sunshine with the harbour at our feet. Then we might relax for a while before we——' he stopped as if struck by a sudden thought, 'well, I might just keep that part as a surprise,' he said, and grinned wickedly at her expectant face. 'Then tomorrow we'll pack a picnic lunch and cross the harbour again and go to the Zoo. You know, I always loved Taronga Park. I've just realised I've been wanting to go back there,' he shrugged, and grinned ruefully, 'not so much to see the animals but to lie in the grass under the trees up above the harbour and just absorb the peace and the beauty of it. What do you say to those ideas?'

Sasha took a deep breath and another of those warnings flashed in her brain like a sign on a highway. Stop! Go back! But then she thought of how he had looked last night and she wondered if two days of this kind of relaxation wouldn't help to ease his burdens just a little.

'I think it sounds perfect,' she said seriously, and made the most conscious effort she ever had to relax herself. She wrinkled her nose and said, 'But I don't know what you've got against the animals at Taronga Park. I think they're lovely. So you better be prepared to be dragged around to see a few of them! Shall we . . . leave the dishes for Mrs Morris and just go?' she added mischievously. 'I'd adore to have a swim as soon as possible. And I bet I can get ready before you!' She jumped up and flashed him a teasing grin, then skipped out of the room as if she had not a care in the world.

She didn't see the look of admiration that came to his eyes as he watched her go.

Sasha sat back and patted her stomach. They were sitting on the deck of Sydney's most famous seafood restaurant, Doyle's, with the waters of Rose Bay lapping at their feet almost. They both wore shorts and T-shirts and had salt-streaked hair and burnt noses.

'Now that's what I call superb,' she said as she eyed the shell from which she had spooned the last of her Lobster Thermidor. 'Do you think . . .?'

'No,' Heath said definitely. 'If you're thinking of a second helping, don't, Funny-face, because you might burst.'

'I wasn't thinking of a second lobster,' she protested indignantly. Then she rolled her eyes and deepened her voice. 'But I haf to confess, Herr Townsend, I *was* wondering about those lovely-looking cheesecakes?' she finished in a high voice and as if she had a plum in her mouth.

He laughed at her. 'And I haf to confess, Fräulein Derwent,' he said, mimicking her, 'that I can't help wondering if one day you don't end up fat.'

'You're right,' she said with a sigh, and reached for her wine glass. 'But I'm not really a glutton. These just happen to be two of my very favourite dishes, you see.'

'I do see,' he said with a grin and a signal to the waitress.

And Sasha started to laugh as he ordered two cheesecakes. 'Now go on, admit it,' she said delightedly. 'You couldn't resist them either!'

'I most certainly could,' he said haughtily. 'It was just that on second thoughts, I couldn't imagine you getting fat. You have too much energy for one thing.'

'Thanks for them kind words,' she said placidly as she slid her spoon into the dessert. 'I can now eat this with a clear conscience. But talking of energy, who was it who forced me to swim and surf until I nearly dropped? Not that I didn't enjoy it, but you're a hard man to keep up with.'

'Ah, but you see you don't know what I've got planned for this afternoon, Blossom.'

'What?' she asked with a comically fearful look on her face.

'Well, I fully intend to . . .' He looked at her with his eyes sparkling wickedly.

'Go on!'

'Drop on to the settee as soon as I get home and sleep for hours. And I reckon you should take a nap too,' he said casually. 'You want to be fresh for tonight.'

She thought for a moment. 'What *is* on tonight?'

'Wait and see.' He smiled at her tantalisingly.

'Oh, please, Heath!'

But he wouldn't be budged. 'Content yourself with the knowledge that you'll enjoy it. And you were right,' he added with a grin, 'I couldn't resist the cheesecakes either. Come on, shall we walk home?'

'Not on your life!' she told him. 'Unless you fancy carrying me?'

Sasha slept deeply and dreamlessly for hours. In fact it was the tinkling of the door chimes that woke them both as the shadows were lengthening outside, and if it hadn't been for daylight saving it, would have been dark already.

It was the building's commissionaire who stood at the door with several striped boxes in his hands.

'They come much earlier, Mr Townsend, like I told you, but I just haven't had a chance to bring 'em up. Burst pipe in number twenty-two,' he added confidingly.

Heath tipped him and turned to Sasha, who was standing behind him now. 'For you,' he said.

'Is this the surprise?' she asked, still faintly flushed from sleep.

'Well, part of it,' he said. 'Actually I ordered them yesterday, but it took some time for them to find exactly what I wanted. It was,' he hesitated, 'meant to be a bonus for helping me out at such short notice yesterday. However, it will do very well for tonight. Open them.'

She hesitated too because she had an inkling that he was watching her very carefully to see how she took the reference to yesterday—traumatic yesterday. She also had an inkling of what was in the boxes, and for a second her mind screamed a protest because it brought back all the agony she had gone through one way and another yesterday. But then she thought, I'm stronger than that, surely? And I set out to achieve something in these two days, didn't I?

She looked up. 'The suspense is killing me,' she said lightly. 'I'll open them in the lounge.'

And despite her reservations, which she was battening down so firmly, the contents of the boxes quite took her breath away, and she gasped as she drew out the most exquisite black cocktail dress, black satin evening shoes and a tiny velvet-covered box. Her mother's evening bag was in another packet.

'Oh, Heath! It's beautiful,' she said genuinely as she held the dress up. 'Thank you so much. What's this?' she asked huskily as she fingered the velvet box.

'Open it,' he said quietly, still watching her closely.

The box contained a set of delicate gold earrings. Sasha blinked and swallowed as she looked at them.

'Thank you,' she said. 'I love them.' She swallowed again. 'But you've overestimated my overtime, I think. And my bag! I forgot about it,' she said with grimace.

'I'm beginning to think I might have under . . .' He stopped abruptly and she spoke quickly.

'Anyway, I'm glad you did. But please tell me before I burst with curiosity—what is this mysterious event tonight?'

Heath sat back and said with an odd glint in his eyes. 'Is it or is it not true that you're a Gilbert and Sullivan freak, Sasha?'

'You know I am,' she said with a grin, and took a deep breath. 'I am the very model of a modern major gen-er-al,' she sang.

He winced laughingly. 'I wonder how many times I've heard you sing that in the shower! Perhaps, after tonight, you'll be able to increase your repertoire.'

'Do you mean . . . you don't mean . . .?'

'I do. *The Mikado* at the Opera House tonight. I've read that it's an excellent production.'

'Oh, Heath!' Sasha jumped up and quite spontaneously flung her arms round his neck. 'Oh thank you! You're an absolute honey.' She kissed him unselfconsciously and he lifted her off her feet and twirled her through the air.

'So are you,' he said laughingly. 'I'm pleased you're pleased.' He put her down, and then the unaffected moment changed subtly. She thought later it was the feel of his hands on her waist, on her skin where her blouse had ridden up. But it wasn't only that, she realised. It was a combination of so many things. His long, powerful legs beneath his canvas shorts. The smooth tanned skin of his shoulders and the ease with which he had lifted her so that she felt as light as thistledown. But most of all, just because he was Heath, the most beautiful tiger in the jungle, and the nicest, she thought with despair.

They stood like that, seemingly both unable to make the move to break free. And her breath came a little faster as she saw the expression in his dark blue eyes change in the instant before he lowered his eyelids to mask it.

Then she was free and he turned away to say casually, 'Hey, we haven't got much time. And I'd like to bet I can get ready before you this time!'

It did take Sasha longer to get ready. But not only because she had more to do, as much as because her hands seemed to be unsure of themselves and her whole body invaded by an inner trembling as she thought of how Heath had looked at her for that brief instant. As a man, not a friend, not in a brotherly way at all. Just as a man assessing a woman and finding her desirable.

'Perhaps I imagined it,' she told herself as she stepped out of the shower. 'And even if I didn't, what difference does it make? It doesn't change anything, Sasha. Besides, I *must* have imagined it.'

The black dress fitted perfectly and managed to combine femininity and chic. And her skin did look pearly beneath it, as he had predicted, beneath the black lace that covered her shoulders and arms right down to the wrists from above the heart-shaped bodice that was formed by the taffeta lining. The skirt was full—a cloud of lace and taffeta about her legs encased in sheer Christian Dior tights, he had thought of everything—and the shoes were the very essence of elegance, with sling-backs, narrow toes and slender, very high heels.

She looked at herself critically in the mirror and then decided to put her hair up so that she could show off her new earrings. That took a bit of extra time, too, but when she finally stood in front of Heath, it was piled smoothly on top of her head with a few wisps coaxed around her face.

'I feel like a different person,' she said lightly as she

accepted his inspection, having once more done battle with her nerves and her curious, foolish fancies. *And* suppressed the thrill that the sight of him, tall and sleek in a black dinner suit with the dark gold of his hair tamed, had brought her.

She turned round slowly so that her skirt flared out and added mischievously, 'I'm also taller, and I think I should warn you, this new Sasha Derwent expects to be treated with much deference tonight. In other words,' she added as she came back to face him and see the slow smile creeping into his eyes, 'I shall be very offended if you call me Funny-face or Blossom or tell me I'll get fat. Because I feel like a princess!' she finished triumphantly, but added wryly, 'thanks to you.'

'You look like one,' said Heath very seriously but with his lips twitching. He held out his arm to her grandly. 'May I have the honour, Miss Derwent, of escorting you to the Opera House? Or perhaps I should call you Ma'am?'

'Just call me Sasha,' she said, grinning as she accepted his arm and they swept towards the door. 'Oh, Heath, I'm really looking forward to this!'

'So am I. Hang on. What about your glasses? Or isn't it done for princesses to be seen out with glasses?'

'I've got my lenses on ... in, whatever's the right term. I can see from here to ... Bondi,' she said grandly and untruthfully.

'Well, I doubt that,' he said laconically. 'But didn't you say they were irritating you?'

'They were, but they're not any more. Look, will you stop worrying about my eyes! That's in the same category as worrying about my weight or calling me silly names,' she said indignantly.

'All right! I shall desist,' he said laughingly. 'After you, ma'am.'

'What are you thinking about, Sasha?'

'Last night. Today. How much I enjoyed the music. How lovely it was lying in the grass watching all the yachts on the harbour. How sweet those little lion cubs were.' Sasha looked up from where she was sitting, leaning over the arm of the settee with her chin resting on both her hands formed into fists as she watched the sun set. 'It's been perfect, hasn't it?'

His dark blue eyes searched her face. They'd been home about half an hour and had both collapsed laughing in the lounge, protesting exhaustion until Heath had roused himself to pour them each a reviver in the form of a long, cool, cocktail which they had sipped in a companionable silence.

He ruffled her hair affectionately and said simply, 'I'm glad.'

'Has it been ... good for you?' she asked hesitantly.

'My dear, it's been the best thing that could have happened to me,' he said. 'You'll never know how much I needed this ... break.'

'I'm so glad,' she said at last when she could find her voice. She stood up. 'I'll make us something to eat. But I warn you, I'm doing nothing more strenuous this evening than watching television, and that only for a while. Because it's back to the ranch tomorrow, and I guess you know what that means—for both of us,' she said humorously. 'Your dear mama won't be in the best of tempers, I guess.'

'Sasha.' He caught her hand as she went to move past him and a cold finger of fear touched her heart, because there was something in his voice—something that filled her with foreboding.

She looked up at him mutely.

'I'm not going back with you tomorrow. I'm leaving tonight.'

'Tonight?' she whispered involuntarily.

'In about half an hour's time,' he said gently as his thumb unthinkingly stroked the inside of her wrist.

'On an assignment?' She stared at him with her heart pounding in her throat, her mouth suddenly dry and every nerve-ending in her body protesting violently.

'. . . You could say so. I'm flying to Melbourne tonight . . .' He stopped.

'Well, I can drive you to the airport,' she said uncertainly at the same time as she thought, The pain! How can I deal with this? Why didn't I expect it?

'No,' he said abruptly, and then more gently, 'No. But tomorrow—you could drive my car home. It'll be more comfortable than taking the train.'

Her mind reacted to this as if she had received a blow, but the knowledge that he was something of an expert at reading her mind made her make one last incredible effort.

'So it's goodbye,' she said unevenly. 'I mean, I guess we'll still see each other . . .'

'Not for a while. But sure we will,' said Heath very quietly. 'Sasha?'

She stared up at him, her naked grey eyes wide and although she didn't know it tinged with an faint final expectancy.

And his fingers tightened unthinkingly on her wrist before he forced himself to loosen his grasp and smile then, but just a little as if it hurt him. 'Thank you. For just being yourself, Napoleon. And don't . . . don't throw yourself away on just anyone, will you?' He leant forward to rest his lips on her forehead for a moment.

'I won't,' she promised in a voice totally unlike her own. 'Don't you either,' she added gruffly.

Heath looked at his watch. 'I better start packing.'

'Oh, I'll give you a hand,' the strange person who had invaded Sasha Derwent's body said. And it was that stranger who got through the next half hour on her behalf. It was a rushed half hour too, for which she was immensely grateful but couldn't help wondering if he'd planned it that way. But finally the door was closed behind him and the cheerful, helpful stranger departed too, leaving only Sasha Derwent, who couldn't believe anything could hurt so much as just watching Heath Townsend leave.

CHAPTER FOUR

THE next morning the sun was gone in reality, and in Sasha's heart too. In the dark, dead hours of the night while Heath was winging his way away from her, she'd tried to console herself with the thought that he could have been right. Of course he was! She'd get over this. She wasn't Sasha Derwent for nothing . . .

And she had stopped to smile sadly as she remembered that this particular saying had been her father's for as long as she could remember and he had used it when she had fallen over as a baby, fallen off her horse somewhat older . . . and when her mother had died. And she thought longingly then of her father, who had been just as devastated as she had, but had never closed her out in his own misery. If I could tell you about all this, Dad, she thought, I'm sure you'd help me see it in its proper prospective.

But by morning, she had given up trying to tell herself she only had a crush on Heath Townsend. Instead, her mind seemed to have gone blank, and she packed her clothes slowly, taking extra care with the black dress, although she left the smoky grey one behind.

And because it was raining, she drove slowly and carefully down the choked confines of Victoria Road in Heath's car, very gradually leaving Sydney and all its memories behind her.

And because she felt a curious numbness, even when she was far out of town with the traffic left behind and the rain stopped, she still drove at the same even speed, uncaring that she was taking almost twice as long over this drive than necessary and that her employer would be in a cadenza by now.

For a few minutes she did ponder how Stephanie Townsend would have reacted to Heath's imperious phone-call—apart from the fact of the inconvenience it represented. But all Heath had said was that Sasha had decided to take the weekend off and had asked him to let her know.

Then, finally, there was no way she could any longer delay driving up the jacaranda-lined driveway to the impressive old house. But while she was prepared for Stephanie's censure, which anyway generally masked a genuine affection for whoever it was heaped upon, she was quite unprepared for the white-faced, tearful Stephanie who rushed out to greet her.

'He's gone crazy!' Stephanie declared furiously as she eyed the car. 'Why did you let him do it, Sasha?' she demanded.

'Do what?' Sasha asked anxiously as she mounted the steps. 'Who?'

'Heath! Who else?'

'I don't understand. Do what?' she asked again.

Stephanie stared at her. 'Do you mean he didn't tell you? And by the way, where have you been this weekend?' She shrugged impatiently. 'But you were at the party with him on Friday, at least, weren't you? Did he say anything? Give you any kind of a hint that this was brewing?'

'Stephanie, I don't know what you're talking about,' Sasha said, but with that feeling of foreboding again in her heart.

'This,' Stephanie said distractedly, and picked up a newspaper from the wicker table on the verandah. She thrust it into Sasha's face and waited impatiently as Sasha scanned the headlines and then trembled as she recognised Heath staring out at her from the front page.

'Oh no!' she exclaimed, going pale.

'Oh yes,' Stephanie said tartly. 'It seems he flew down

to Melbourne last night and told them he was not renewing his contract with the channel, dragged the top brass from their beds last night, mind you, to do it. And then he flew out of Australia.'

Sasha's knees buckled and she sat down in the nearest chair. 'But how could he do that?' she whispered.

'He persuaded them to take some man in his place and let him take the leave that was due to him to take him up to the end of his present contract. Some man called ... Havelock. Apparently he's been doing this kind of thing overseas.'

Sasha's mouth dropped open. 'Brent Havelock?' she asked incredulously.

'Something like that,' Stephanie said impatiently, then wiped her eyes and sniffed desolately. 'I suppose he left a note at the flat for you to bring the car home? But I didn't even get a note. All I got was a telegram ... telling me he was going back to "pure" journalism, whatever that is,' she added viciously.

Oh, no! was Sasha's most coherent thought. Then, oh heavens! Why did I do it? Why did I say all those *silly* things on Friday night at the party? And why didn't he tell me?

'Of course I know why he didn't tell me,' Stephanie said tearfully, unconsciously echoing Sasha's thoughts. 'Because when Heath makes up his mind to do anything he doesn't consult anyone, least of all me! In case I put up a fight. Which I would have. Does he really think I don't know what he means by "pure" journalism?' she asked illogically. 'I know exactly what it means. It means finding the blackest, cruellest war he can, as if singlehandedly he could right all the wrongs in this world.'

'Where?' Sasha's voice came out as a croak.

'He didn't say,' Stephanie wept. 'But you can bet your bottom dollar it will be something like El Salvador or somewhere just as bad. Oh, Sasha!'

Sasha stared at the elegant, silver-haired woman and saw a grief that matched her own. Although in some respects Heath and his mother were too alike to be compatible in each other's company for very long, she knew Stephanie was tremendously fond, tremendously proud of her only son. And the deep hurt and anxiety she was feeling touched Sasha despite her own pain, so that she stood up and put her arms around Stephanie.

'Don't cry,' she whispered. 'He'll be back.' Please God, let him be back, she prayed.

'But I had such . . . plans to tell him about, Sasha,' Stephanie sobbed.

'What plans?' Sasha said gently. 'Tell me.'

Stephanie tensed, then pulled away and blew her nose. Finally she patted Sasha on the cheek affectionately and made a great effort to control herself. 'I will one day,' she said. 'Because you're just like the daughter I . . .' She stopped and took a breath and then went on, 'And you mustn't look so upset yourself. I know you look upon Heath almost as an elder brother. But you're right, he'll be back, pet.' She laughed shakily. 'What a pair we are!' She tucked Sasha's hand into hers and led her inside. 'I was going to say what we need is a cup of tea, but on second thoughts, I reckon a good stiff drink is what *I* need. Seen your father yet?' she asked over her shoulder.

'No. I thought I'd pop over the fence after lunch.'

'Good,' said Stephanie with something of her former briskness. 'And when you do, ask him if he's got a minute to come up and see me. I feel as if I could do with some of his . . . common sense.'

It was a strange week that followed. To all intents and purposes, the household got back to normal and Stephanie recovered her composure completely. In fact the only time she mentioned Heath was one day during their morning break as they sipped coffee on the verandah just above the rose garden.

She said out of the blue, 'It's a strange thing about Heath. He bullies me shamefully, never listens to a word I say and quite breaks my heart sometimes, but I always feel a little less alive when he's not around, as you've no doubt gathered,' she added with a wry twist to her lips.

She caught Sasha's eye and they both grinned.

'But the funniest part is,' Stephanie went on, 'I'm supposed to be a very enlightened woman. Some most kind person even once compared me to Emily Pankhurst ... yet I really have only one burning ambition left. And that's to see Heath find the right woman, marry her, be happy with her, and have children with her. Not only—well, it's a little like a call of the wild, I've discovered—to want to see your grandchildren but because, whatever she might think to the contrary, I think he'd make a very good husband.'

Oh, so do I, Sasha thought, but didn't say it. She couldn't find anything to say, she found, and when she at last looked up from her cup, it was to see Stephanie staring at her concernedly, so that her heart tripped and she wondered if she'd given herself away.

But all Stephanie said was, 'You know you don't look very well, Sasha. I noticed it the other day. I think you might need a tonic. Growing girls often do.'

Sasha winced inwardly but said gravely, 'I think I might have stopped growing a few years back, Stephanie. I'll be nineteen in a week or two.'

They laughed at that. 'True,' said Stephanie. 'It's a strange thing, but the older one gets, the younger young people look to you. I expect thirty or so years hence you'll notice the phenomenon too. All the same, you do look a bit peaky. Is there any problem?'

Sasha thought. 'Well, I've had a couple of headaches,' she said hoping desperately this would cover her. 'Perhaps you're right,' she added. 'Maybe I am growing in a way. I'll go and see Doctor James. But you know what he'll prescribe, don't you?' She wrinkled her nose. 'Liver!'

'A very good source of iron, so I'm told,' said Stephanie with a grin. 'But you do that, Sasha. Because he's really not such an old fogey, you know. Why, I believe he delivered you into this world!'

'That's what I mean,' Sasha said. 'And he is an old fogey, but I love him just the same. Although sometimes he treats me as *his* baby.'

'I'm afraid we all do, dear. But only because we love you.'

How right you are, Stephanie, Sasha said to herself. 'Stephanie . . .?' she began.

'Yes, pet?'

'Oh, nothing. Well, I only wondered if you ever grow out of feeling—sort of unsure of yourself?'

'No,' said Stephanie after a long pause. 'Up until quite recently I thought, yes. Then I discovered that in one field at least, human relationships—well, no.'

She's thinking of Heath, Sasha thought. Isn't it curious that we should both be thinking, always thinking of Heath? My goodness! How long does it take to forget Heath?

She said, 'I thought not.'

'Sasha?'

'Yes?'

'You're growing into one of the loveliest young women I've ever seen. Physically and mentally,' Stephanie said sincerely. 'Remember that, when you feel a little unsure, won't you? And don't . . .' she hesitated.

'I won't,' said Sasha with a mischievous grin, and thought, heavens, I'm also growing into a consummate actress! 'I mean, I won't fall for the first or the second or the third man I meet. So don't worry.'

Stephanie looked at her curiously. 'How did you know I was going to say that?'

'Oh well,' Sasha said airily but turning faintly pink, 'that's the kind of advice I seem to be getting these days. I'm sure it's very good advice,' she added hastily to cover the slight cynicism in her voice.

Stephanie was thoughtful for a minute, then she grinned suddenly. 'One forgets,' she said, 'what bothersome old bores one's elders can be. Oh well,' she stretched, 'should we get back to work? Or should we take the rest of the day off? I'm quite in the mood to be lazy.'

It was Sasha's turn to look curious, for this was not quite in character with the Stephanie she knew. She said, 'I think we are as much behind as we could get, aren't we?'

'Blossom, you're quite right. All right, drag me back to work, you slavedriver!'

Mike Gibson rang up the next morning. His parents owned a property in the district and he and Sasha had got to know each other through mutual friends about twelve months ago. She often wondered what had been the turning point for Mike, because for many months it had been a simple, uncomplicated friendship, spent mostly in the company of others. But lately it had changed and Mike had adopted a subtly proprietorial attitude towards Sasha, so that now most of their dates were tête-à-tête and she got the distinct feeling she had allowed herself to drift into becoming Mike's 'girl' without quite knowing how it had happened.

But two things moved her to alter that impression as she spoke to him on the phone. The first was the faintly petulant note of chiding in his voice as he attempted to grill her about the weekend she had spent in town. Almost as if she was a witness being cross-examined. The second thing was the uncomfortable memory of Heath's summing up of Mike, which although she hadn't admitted it at the time—the first time, rather, she thought, and went pink—had nailed him rather accurately.

So that all this, together with the memories Mike was evoking with his persistent questions, made her more brusque perhaps than she intended to be. 'You don't own me, Mike,' she said coldly into the phone at last. 'I went into town because Heath needed me and I decided to stay the weekend. Quite simple really. And it's not as if we had a date that I broke, is it?'

There was a short silence on the other end. Then he said thoughtfully, 'I'd beware of Heath if I were you, Sasha. I know you work for his mother and all that, but—' he hesitated, 'well, it's very easy to get a sort of . . . tarnished reputation, if you know what I mean.'

'No, I don't, Mike!' she said indignantly. 'Are you accusing me . . .' She stopped short and closed her eyes. Oh brother! she thought. If only he knew how right he was. And here am I . . .

Mike's voice cut across her thoughts. 'I'm not accusing you of anything, Sasha. All I'm saying is you have to be careful with a man like Heath who has a reputation for . . .'

'Gobbling up little girls like me?' she said sweetly into the phone, although her eyes were bright with rage. 'Well, let me tell you something, Mike, Heath wouldn't harm a hair of my head—unfortunately. But if ever he crooked his little finger at me, I'd go like a shot!'

She heard the smothered exclamation at the other end of the line and smiled. 'What was that you said?' she asked innocently.

It was a moment before he replied. 'Look, Sasha,' he said finally, 'you've taken this all wrong.'

'Have I?' she said flatly.

'*Yes!* You don't understand.'

'But I do,' she said wearily. 'I'm sorry, Mike, I don't think we're going to see eye to eye over this and probably a lot of other things. So I think it's best if we

don't see each other any more. I'm sorry,' she said
again, and put the phone down decisively just as a
movement behind her made her jump.

She turned to see her father standing behind her. 'Oh,
Dad!' she said weakly. 'You gave me a fright!'

The tall, distinguished, silver-haired man in front of
her smiled and patted her head. 'What's to be so sorry
about?' he asked with a twinkle in his eye. 'And who
don't you think'll ever see eye to eye with you?'

'Mike Gibson,' she said with a little sigh, and added
reproachfully, 'I thought you told me it just wasn't
done to creep up on people and listen to their
conversations.'

'Did I? Ah well, when you get to my age you can
disregard your own advice.' They laughed together.
Then he said more soberly, 'Don't think I'm prying, but
you sounded pretty upset. That's why I . . . inadvertently
found myself listening. Did Mike do something
objectionable to make you so angry?'

Sasha sighed and twisted her hands. 'Not really,' she
said. 'I suppose he can't help being who he is.'

'And that's . . . not the right person for you?' her
father said acutely.

'Uh-huh.'

He watched for a moment with narrowed eyes. 'Then
you should be feeling relieved, Sasha,' he said gently,
'instead of looking a picture of misery. By the way, I
must admit I agree with you—about Mike. It's a
strange thing, but very young men are often a lot less
mature than women of the same age.'

Sasha looked up at him with parted lips.

'What is it?' he asked.

'Oh . . .' Sasha shrugged, 'nothing. Just that someone
else told me something like that only—only a few days
ago.'

She coloured as her father's gaze sharpened, and
thought, now is the time to tell him. But she found she

couldn't frame the words somehow. Perhaps because Jonathan Derwent and Heath were very good friends. If it had been a stranger, it might be easier, she mused. But how to tell him of her feelings for Heath when she knew they admired each other, man to man?

So she took a breath and made herself say gaily, 'What brings you to this neck of the woods, Papa? Come to see me or to scrounge some of Cookie's scones? It is nearly tea-time,' she added with a whimsical smile as she glanced at her watch.

It seemed he hesitated before he grinned at her and rumpled her hair again. 'Both, my dear daughter.'

It was on Sunday evening, a week exactly after Heath had gone, that Stephanie said to Sasha, 'Could you ask Cookie to chill a bottle of champagne for dinner, pet?'

Sasha wrinkled her nose. 'Whose birthday?' she asked.

'Does there have to be a birthday to have champagne?'

'I suppose not. Yes, I'll ask her.'

But when she walked into the dining room that night she stopped and frowned. The beautiful old silky-oak table gleamed beneath its silver and china.

'Something's up,' she muttered to herself. 'Not only champagne but the best china.'

'Sasha! There you are, dear.'

She turned as her father came into the room and gave her a quick hug.

'Dad! You again? You must be the mystery dinner guest.'

'You could say so. Or just the man who came to dinner and . . .'

'What's this about a mystery?' asked Stephanie as she swept into the room looking magnificent. And she and Jonathan Derwent exchanged looks of pure mischief.

'All right, you two,' Sasha said resignedly. 'Out with it!'

'Er—this might be a good time to open the champagne, Jonathan,' said Stephanie.

'Couldn't be a better one,' Sasha's father said happily, and reached for the bottle that stood invitingly in a frosted silver bucket.

'I *know*,' Sasha exclaimed, suddenly enlightened. 'That Ambassadorship you were telling me about that you were thinking of accepting if it came your way. Oh, congratulations, Stephanie!' she said warmly.

But it was a strange little silence that greeted her words and Sasha realised that her father and her employer both looked slightly uncomfortable.

'It's not that?' she said at last, more confused than ever.

'No, Sasha,' Stephanie said gently. 'I wonder if we haven't handled this badly,' she added quietly, then took a deep breath. 'In fact I'm retiring from politics, Sasha. And we were rather sure you'd worked out the reason . . .'

'Well, I obviously haven't,' Sasha said helplessly, and then was struck by a strange thought. She looked at her father to see him staring at her steadily. 'You don't mean . . .?' She left her question in the air.

He nodded. 'Stephanie's done me the honour of consenting to marry me,' he said gently. 'We had hoped to have your blessing,' he added very soberly.

For an instant she didn't know whether to laugh or cry with pleasure.

'Oh . . . darlings!' she said at last beneath their anxious gazes. 'Oh, I'm so happy for you both! I couldn't think of anything more perfect! But I swear I didn't have an inkling . . . although I should have,' she added as a host of small recollections flooded her mind. 'I don't know how I could have been so blind. Oh, Dad!' She hugged her father and spilt champagne all down his jacket, then turned to Stephanie.

'You don't . . . I mean, I thought you might resent me a little,' Stephanie said anxiously. 'I know how much you loved your mother. But it's not that I would ever want to supplant her in your heart or your father's.'

'You could never do that, Stephanie,' Sasha said very gently. 'Because you have a very special place of your own, you see.' She took the older woman's hand and pressed it, then they hugged each other and more champagne was spilt, and a few happy tears too.

Until Sasha said, 'Darlings, I've just been struck by a thought, though. As one who knows,' she grinned impishly at them both, 'do you realise you are two of the most impossible people to get on with first thing in the mornings?'

Stephanie gave a shout of laughter. 'As one who knows, my dear, I thought you might have reserved that title for Heath.'

'Oh, he's not really . . .' Sasha stopped abruptly and then pressed on. 'I mean, it's only when he's had a heavy night. I mean, he can also be impossibly bright and energetic too, can't he?' she added, and forced a rueful smile to her lips.

And he can be unbelievably sweet and funny and just so beautiful, and he can make you laugh and want to cry at the same time . . .

'Does he know?' she asked, as much to break the chain of her memories as anything. Then she was back to reality. 'Of course not,' she answered her own question. 'I'm so sorry,' she said quietly to Stephanie.

A shadow crossed Stephanie's face. 'I did so want him to be at the wedding,' she said with an effort. 'But after all,' she added with an attempt at lightheartedness, 'he's been urging me to take a man for years,' she grinned at Sasha's father, 'and he could be away for *years*, so we decided to go ahead as we'd planned.'

'When is the great day?' Sasha asked hurriedly to still

her erratic heart beat at the thought of not seeing Heath for years.

'A week today,' her father said. 'That is if you'd do us the honour of sharing your birthday with our wedding day?'

'I'd love to,' she said simply.

It was a rushed week and for the most part a happy one.

Sasha resolutely pushed Heath to the back of her mind as she and Stephanie went about the business of tying up her political career. In this they were aided by Stephanie's parliamentary secretary, Edith West, a formidable woman in her fifties who adored Stephanie. And it was Edith who let the cat out of the bag and caused the one disturbance in that week.

Jonathan and Stephanie had told Sasha they planned to go to the Great Barrier Reef for their honeymoon.

'Lucky . . . lucky them!' said Sasha on another dismal rainy day.

'Yes,' Edith replied. 'And if you ask me, much more sensible than traipsing around the world for a year,' she addded, being one of the breed who considered even New Zealand a dangerously foreign place.

'What do you mean?' asked Sasha after a moment.

Edith looked slightly uncomfortable, and then more so as Stephanie walked in and Sasha turned to her.

'What's this I hear about you and Dad wanting to go round the world, Stephanie?' she asked. 'It sounds a great idea! And I know Dad's been wanting to do something like that for ages.'

Stephanie shot Edith an annoyed look and said, 'Well, we plan to get round to it one day, but not just yet.'

'But why not?' Sasha demanded, and chose just that moment to empty out a desk drawer from which fell a passport and a whole lot of travel brochures together with a tourist agency brochure and cancelled itinerary dated from the date of the wedding. She stared down at all this and then lifted her face to Stephanie.

'Oh no!' she said threateningly. 'You're not going because of me, is that it?'

Stephanie looked helpless for a moment. Then she said placatingly, 'Blossom . . .'

'Don't you "Blossom" me!' snapped Sasha with the light of battle squarely in her eyes. 'I've been treated like a baby for long enough by all of you. Do you honestly believe I can't take care of myself?'

'Sasha—look, pet, it's not that, but you'll probably want to look for another job, for one thing, and for another . . .' Stephanie stopped and sighed.

'What?'

'To be quite honest, we wouldn't have minded so much if Heath had been here to keep an eye on you,' Stephanie said desperately.

Sasha nearly laughed hollowly at the awful irony of this. But she managed to say steadily, 'Assuming I do have to have someone to keep an eye on me, Edith will be here, won't she? Won't you?' She turned to Edith and then swung back to Stephanie. 'Anyway, before you cancelled your trip, before Heath left, what plans had you made for this place? Were you going to let it out, or what? Because Heath wouldn't have spent much time here.'

Stephanie gritted her teeth. 'No. Er . . . Edith was going to stay here and manage both properties.'

'That's perfect, then!' Sasha cried. 'She can manage me too—as well as anyone else could. Can't you, Edith?'

Edith looked at her warily like someone caught in an unexpected burst of crossfire. Then she said gruffly, 'As well as Heath could, I suspect.'

'Then that's settled,' Sasha said determinedly. She reached for the phone and checked the number on the brochure.

And she remained adamant even when Stephanie called her father up. So adamant that they finally gave in, although right up to the last minute, when they were due to board their plane, having exchanged their vows in the beautiful old rose garden at home, they were still clucking over her anxiously.

Until she said finally, 'I promise I'll write to you regularly, wherever you are. Now will you get on that plane and forget about me!' Then she relented. 'Please, just be happy, because it makes me so happy to see you two together like this!'

CHAPTER FIVE

SASHA stared at the letter she was writing. She nibbled the end of her pen and noted the date she'd put at the top with a tinge of surprise. For it was exactly six months to the day since Stephanie and her father had married. She also noted that she was nineteen years and six months old precisely now.

Six months which had seen a lot of changes in her life.

'Six months,' she murmured out loud with a faint smile, 'during which I managed to get myself a very good job, not get run over by a bus or taken advantage of by any strange men—or any familiar men, for that matter. And yes, say it, Sasha,' she urged herself, 'six months and two weeks since you last saw or heard from Heath.' She flinched and added, 'Oh, shut up! Forget about Heath and think about Brent.'

She laid her pen down and let her mind roam back to that incredible day a week after her father and Stephanie had left, when she had come into town for a job interview and bumped into, of all people, Brent Havelock.

Sasha had been embarrassed and flustered as she had once again recalled all the things she had said that fateful night of the party. But Brent had calmly overridden her desire to get away from him as fast as she could and steered her into a coffee shop. And to her surprise he had managed to put her so much at her ease that she had found herself telling him all that had happened to her lately and how she was looking for a job. But he had taken her breath away when he had said immediately that it so happened he was looking for an assistant and offered her the position.

She had stared at him open-mouthed. 'After what I said that night?' she had asked faintly. 'Surely . . .'

'Well, a lot of it was true, but . . .'

'Was it?' she interrupted. 'If you only knew how much I regretted saying those things! And if there was any truth, I aimed it at Veronica and everyone else travelling on her bandwagon. But who did I hit?' she said bitterly. 'Only Heath. And he has more compassion in his little finger than the rest of them put together.' Her voice was husky with emotion.

Brent had sat forward. 'I wondered about that,' he had said thoughtfully. 'If what you said had anything to do with him going like that. Veronica, in her own inimitable manner, maintained it was because of her. And I think in all fairness, for the first time in her life, she was quite cut up about it. But she also reckoned he'll come back to her sooner or later.'

'He . . . he might,' Sasha had agreed painfully. 'I never pretended to take all the credit for his going.'

Something in Brent's gaze had sharpened then and she'd looked away quickly. But he had only gone on to explain to her that he had agreed to fill Heath's shoes only temporarily. And what he had really come back to Australia to do was a television series on Australia and Papua New Guinea for an overseas television company. 'What I would need you for, Sasha, is really more of a research position. Someone to do the Australian groundwork for me. It would mean a lot of travel, quite a bit of it on your own, a lot of exploring and a lot of fun, I should think . . .'

Sasha came back to the present with a laugh gurgling in her throat as she recalled some of the places she had 'explored' and some of the fixes she had got herself into. But it had been a lot of fun, in fact Brent's job had been a lifesaver, and now the groundwork for a series of ten programmes had been laid and they were set to get down to the serious business of filming.

But if you're honest, Sasha, she thought, you have to admit it's not only Brent's job that's been a lifesaver, but Brent himself.

Their friendship had blossomed not only because it was heaven to have someone to talk to about Heath occasionally, someone who knew him and had known him for years. And yet ...

She got up and moved restlessly across to the window of the small, comfortable flat she now rented in town. If you're honest you have to admit too, Sasha, that Brent wants to step over the line of friendship now. And therein lies a problem.

She sighed and rested her head against the cool glass. She liked Brent so much, and some days she knew that it was because she liked him so much she could never marry him as a substitute for Heath. But on other days she chided herself that she wasn't giving Brent or herself a chance. Perhaps he could erase Heath from her heart and mind if only she'd let him try.

She rubbed her temples wearily and her eyes strayed back to the letter she was writing to Stephanie and her father, who were now in Peru. And she couldn't help a faint twitching of her lips as she remembered what she had gone through to get them to go on this trip while now it seemed as if they might stay away for ever.

Still, she told herself, with Edith managing both properties so successfully—which she discovered anew, every time she managed to get home for a weekend— and she herself with such a stimulating job, there was no need for them to worry about home.

'Which is just as it should be,' she muttered to herself with a grin that intensified as she pictured her ultra-conservative father and her elegant stepmother climbing the Andes ...

The phone rang beside her, disturbing her thoughts and causing her to glance at her watch in surprise, for it was very late.

'Hello.'

A blood-chilling whisper came down the line. 'Blossom? Is that you?'

'Edith!' said Sasha, and smiled. 'I was just thinking of you.' Her smile faded. 'Is something wrong?'

'Oh, Sasha,' Edith's despairing whisper came down the line, 'I've been trying to get hold of you for days. Where've you been? Never mind. It wasn't easy for me to get to the phone . . .'

Sasha took the receiver from her ear and stared at it nonplussed. Then she replaced it and said, 'I don't understand. Why couldn't you get to the phone?'

'Because he wouldn't let me. He threatened me with all sorts of things if I contacted *anyone*. But I had to. You don't know . . .'

Sasha said dazedly, 'Are you trying to tell me some maniac has you . . . but why aren't you ringing the police, Edith . . . never mind. Look, hang up and I will . . .'

'No, Sasha!' Edith's whisper became more urgent. 'It's not just some maniac. It's Heath!'

'Heath's . . . home?' Sasha went as white as the blouse she wore. 'But how . . . I mean . . .'

'He's home all right,' Edith whispered grimly. 'Has been for nearly a week.' Then she sighed heavily. 'And he's in a bad way, Sasha. What's more, he's planning to leave again, but he's not fit to be going anywhere and I know Stephanie would never forgive me if I let him. But he made me promise . . . not only that,' her voice rose indignantly only to sink again, 'he watches me like a hawk! Sasha, for your new mother's sake, please come and see what you can do. Only don't let him know I rang you. Just make out you popped in unexpectedly.'

Sasha licked her lips. 'I'll be there in a couple of hours. Edith . . .'

'No, come first thing in the morning, pet. He's asleep

now. And remember, when you see him, act surprised.
Oh, thank you, Sasha!' The line died.

Act surprised, Sasha told herself as she drove down that
familiar driveway with the jacarandas now bare and
lifeless-looking, on what was a cold, grey winter's day.

She had been telling herself this throughout the long
drive, to still the inner panic she felt—had felt since she
had put the phone down slowly, her mind seething with
unanswered questions. It had been all she could do to
heed Edith's request to wait until morning, and the
dark, dead hours of the night had dragged unbearably.

But she was here now. She brought her little car to a
halt on the gravel beneath the front verandah and took
a deep breath. Act surprised . . .

She made herself jump out and run up the front
steps, calling lightly as she went, 'Anyone home?' Act
surprised. 'Edith?' she sang out cheerfully. 'It's me—
Blossom! The prodigal child returned!' The front door
stood open and she crossed the threshold into the long,
dark passageway and stopped as the passage lights
sprang on.

'Edith?' she said, but this time tentatively, and
blinked at the sudden radiance. Then she made out the
tall figure leaning against one of the doorways further
down and her heart started to pound. Act surprised,
Sasha, she told herself tremblingly as she started to
walk again, and then thought, I don't have to act . . .

'Heath . . .?' Her voice came out as a strangled
whisper.

He didn't say a word as she advanced towards him
and stumbled once.

Oh, Heath, what have they done to you? her heart
cried as her disbelieving eyes took in the tall figure clad
in blue cord trousers and a blue sweater that matched
his eyes. For this was such a different Heath from her
memories of him—as tall as ever, but somehow gaunt

and with new lines on his face and a pallor that frightened her. But it was his eyes that frightened her even more and made her stop in her tracks.

Those dark blue eyes that she had seen range through so many expressions. But she had never seen this expression in them—not for her. Never seen Heath looking at her with such a blaze of anger in his eyes that she felt scorched and bit her lip hard enough to draw blood.

He didn't straighten up, just looked her up and down and then said in a cold, hard voice, 'I might have known I couldn't trust Edith.'

'I . . . I don't know what you mean,' she faltered. 'Heath, why didn't you let me know you were home?'

'Because I didn't choose to, Sasha,' he said coolly. 'Anyway, I won't be home for long, sweet stepsister, so you may put all your Florence Nightingale instincts back in the box. I presume Edith gave you a full rundown?'

'No,' Sasha whispered, and found her throat painfully restricted, 'she didn't. But I only have to look at you to know . . . you're not well.' She stopped and winced at the flash of blue fire her words brought to his eyes. I shouldn't have said that, she thought dazedly.

Then the fire was gone and in its place a sort of studied cynicism as he seemed to change tack deliberately. 'I've been hearing great things of you, Sasha,' he said casually. 'It looks as if you've got quite a career ahead of you. You must tell me about it. Let's see if we can raise a cup of tea for you. Although I suspect Edith might have bolted in fright,' he added with a curiously unpleasant little smile.

He straightened up then and for the first time Sasha saw the cane in his hand and his knuckles white with effort as he turned slowly and limped painfully down the passage away from her towards the kitchen.

'I'll . . . I'll make the tea,' she said breathlessly as she followed him into the kitchen. She unwound her scarf and took off her gloves, trying not to watch as he sat down awkwardly at the big kitchen table.

'Sasha,' he said abruptly as she filled the kettle, 'please tell me truthfully, did Edith get in touch with you?'

She plugged the kettle in carefully and then turned to look at him. 'Yes, Heath,' she said simply. 'But you mustn't blame her. She was only doing what she felt she had to. And besides, as you mentioned earlier,' she added with her lips twitching, 'we are related now, aren't we? I wonder if that bit of news came as much of a surprise to you as it did to me?'

He looked at her thoughtfully, then shrugged. 'I guess it did. But I'm very happy for them. And that's why I've got to know if she's managed to get in touch with them, as well. Because the very last thing I want on my conscience is for them to come dashing home on my account and Edith's sense of melodrama. I've given my mother enough to worry about over the years.'

'She hasn't,' Sasha said reassuringly. 'But . . .' She hesitated and thought, no, as a strange presentiment took her, I might need that weapon myself. 'But,' she said with an effort, 'she's very worried about you. Won't you tell me how this happened, at least?' She tried to make herself speak as matter-of-factly as she could and poured the tea as she spoke.

Heath folded his arms across his chest and stared down at the teacup she had placed in front of him. Then he lifted his eyes and all she could see was a sort of wry amusement in them. 'I ran out of luck, Blossom, and ran into a couple of bullets. If she wasn't my mother, I imagine that might even give Stephanie an odd sense of satisfaction, because she's been trying to warn me off for long enough, hasn't she? But if you're going to turn maternal on her behalf, Sasha, don't bother. All it needs is a little time and I'll be as good as new.'

He held her gaze deliberately and the mockery in his eyes hurt even more than had the anger she'd seen. She also realised instinctively that he had no intention of telling her any more.

But what surprised her was the intensity of her own physical reaction to this bitter, hard Heath. A longing that almost took her breath away to reach across to him and cradle his dark gold head to her breast, so that she had to look away and clench her hands in her lap.

I thought so, an inner voice murmured. You haven't got over him, have you, Sasha? Maybe you never will.

She cleared her throat. 'Edith . . . said you were going away.' She looked up to find him watching her.

'Yes,' he said after a moment.

'Where?'

'Somewhere warm,' he said idly. 'I thought I might take a protracted cruise.'

'Why did you come home, Heath?' she asked with a catch in her voice.

'I really can't imagine, Sasha,' he said wryly. 'Ostensibly to tie up some business ends that I'd left loose. But it was a mistake. I'm bored to death already. Listen, enough of me. Why don't we have a celebratory hello-goodbye dinner tonight? Then I can hear all your news before you whizz back to the world of television and I head for the wide blue yonder that's beckoning me so insistently. Provided,' he added with a faint grin, 'you can raise Edith from whichever hole she's scuttled into?'

He stood up, and she noticed the beading of sweat the effort brought to his brow.

'What are you going to do?' she asked uncertainly.

'I'm going to spend the day closeted with the telephone,' he said ruefully, 'and via it, my stockbroker, travel agent, etc. See you at dinner, Funny-face,' he added carelessly, and limped out of the room.

Sasha stared across the desk at Doctor James, her face set and determined.

The doctor returned her gaze a little warily over the top of his bi-focals. 'Are you sure he's planning to go away again, Sasha?'

'Quite sure. But even to me—a layman—it's obvious he's in no fit state to be going anywhere. Which is why I came to see you. Edith West tells me you managed to get some information from a specialist Heath consulted when he arrived home.'

'Yes, I did. Miss West seems to be of the same opinion as you—that he'll be leaving again. Which is why I took the liberty of ... making some enquiries. However, Heath is not my patient and I'm rather concerned about meddling in his affairs, Sasha.'

'Well, I'm not,' Sasha said boldly. 'In fact I feel I have an obligation to his mother, who is now also my stepmother, to do all I can for him. But he won't tell me anything, which is why I've come to you. *Is* he in a fit state to be gallivanting on a Pacific cruise or whatever else he's planning?'

Doctor James sighed suddenly. 'Sasha—to be quite honest, no. What he really needs is considerable care and attention, because he has a very trying time ahead of him.'

'In what way?' she asked carefully after a moment.

'For the most part, in the same way anyone convalescing from the injuries he sustained and the operations he underwent. If he looks after himself and takes things slowly, he'll be as good as new. Even his leg will respond to physiotherapy, but these things all take time. But there's one area that's a little more complicated. You see, apparently he sustained a blow to the base of the skull which damaged his optic nerve. And—well, there's some doubt whether the surgery performed was successful.'

For a few moments it seemed to Sasha as if the world

had stopped. She heard no sounds apart from the ticking of the surgery clock. Everything else including the noisy traffic outside the window seemed to be blocked out.

Then she said jerkily, 'Are you ... telling me Heath could go blind?'

'Not necessarily, Sasha,' Doctor James said firmly. 'That's the very darkest prognosis. But that it's a very delicate, tricky area I can't deny. And the important thing now, while they determine whether the nerve is healing or deteriorating, whether he requires further surgery, is peace and quiet for him, lack of strain and to get him as fit as possible.'

'Is he ... but he isn't blind now, is he?' she asked shakily. 'I mean, I didn't notice anything,' she added helplessly.

'No, he's not. But he's experiencing some visual distortions from time to time, consistent with, perhaps, pressure on the nerve.' Doctor James looked down at his hands and then raised his eyes to Sasha. 'My dear, I understand and appreciate your concern. And now that I've told you this, I must confess I feel a little guilty about not taking a more positive approach myself. I count his mother as a very good friend of mine, you see. But if Heath's made up his mind I doubt if there's a great deal you or I can do.'

'Oh yes, there is,' she said very slowly. 'At least, there's something I can do.' She tilted her chin resolutely.

'Well, I wish you good luck. And if you do succeed, having stuck my oar in now, I shall back you to the hilt.'

But that night at dinner Sasha didn't feel quite so resolute.

Edith, who had dispensed with the services of a cook, had made an extra effort with the meal, and the table and the silver shone brilliantly, reminding Sasha of the night her father and Stephanie had broken their news to her, which added a twist of irony to the situation, she thought.

But there were humorous touches to it as well. Edith, particularly, supplied a few. Never loquacious exactly, she went out of her way to be as charming as possible, although she displayed a tendency to glance at Heath occasionally like an anxious mouse in the presence of a cobra.

Not that Heath gave any indication of wanting to pounce on her. In fact he too set out to charm, and from his manner it was hard to believe he had a care in the world. And he skilfully drew Sasha out about her job and the more out-of-the-way places and people she had encountered, so that to all intents and purposes it was a cheerful dinner.

Then Edith pushed back her chair and said goodnight abruptly and the evening seemed to splinter into fragments. Sasha and Heath were left on their own with an unspoken tension lying between them like an invisible cloud.

Heath spoke first after the silence that had attended Edith's departure.

He had changed into a navy silk shirt and a tweed jacket, and Sasha hadn't been able to stop herself from wondering what kind of an ordeal just changing his clothes represented. She herself had chosen a topaz-yellow, fine woollen dress that contrasted brilliantly with her hair and fell in soft graceful folds about her figure as she moved.

'So you and Brent make a good team, by the sound of things,' Heath said abruptly as he toyed with his wine glass. 'I read an article about the two of you and the series.'

'Oh.' Sasha remembered the article and the accompanying picture of her and Brent, and wondered where he had come across it, because she couldn't imagine him being in the habit of reading women's magazines.

'Yes. It should be a very good production.'

She smiled, but a little absently. 'We only have the basics so far. There's a great deal more to go into the melting pot.'

'But you've worked well as a team?' he said, and lowered his eyes in the instant that she realised he was watching her very carefully.

'Oh yes,' she said. 'But I think my period of usefulness has waned now. I found the Australian sites but from here on the experts move in. Scriptwriters—so many different people with talents I don't pretend to have.'

There was another silence. Then he said, not looking at her, 'Sasha, I hope you're not trying to tell me anything.'

'Heath,' she took her courage in both hands, 'I resigned today.'

'Oh no,' he muttered through his teeth.

'Yes,' she said with a calm she was far from feeling.

'Sasha,' he lifted his eyes to hers, 'don't make me say it.' His voice was full of menace and there was a coldness is his eyes that made her shiver inwardly.

But she pressed on. 'Say what?'

'You know bloody well what,' he said contemptuously. 'But if you have to have it spelt out ... I have no intention of letting you sit around here playing nursemaid to me, stepsister. I can find someone far more suitable for that purpose, should I decide I need one. And I can spell out what I mean by suitable if you'd like,' he added coolly but with a slow, insolent glance that mentally stripped her naked and dismissed her so that she had no doubt of what he meant.

She felt the colour rise from the base of her throat and her first impulse was to run from him and her first thought was that she'd never recover from this wound.

But she stifled these reactions and thought of what Doctor James had said.

And she even contrived a faint smile as she said lightly, 'That doesn't sound like a very good idea at the moment. But if there's someone here, someone who'd stay with you?' She looked at him enquiringly and thought she detected a gleam of amusement in his eyes.

He said dryly, 'If you're proposing to solicit on my behalf, Blossom, thank you kindly, but no. I'm well able to take care of those arrangements myself. And I'm *leaving*, Sasha, so let's just forget we had this discussion, shall we?' The amusement was there plainly now. 'There's nothing you can do to stop me, Napoleon,' he added almost gently.

Sasha took a deep breath. 'Yes, there is.'

'Oh?' He lay back in his chair and studied her from beneath half-closed eyelids while his long fingers twirled his wine glass round and round. 'I hope you're not planning to take me by force or . . . deprive me of my clothes, say?' He laughed at her hot face. 'Oh, Sasha . . .'

'*Heath*,' she interrupted desperately, and stopped abruptly. Then she took another deep breath and said, 'You're not going to like this but if you do go, I'll wire your mother and tell her exactly what's happened to you. Do you know what that will do to her?' she asked steadily. 'Have you any idea how upset she was when you left last time? Well, I'll tell you, she was brokenhearted, Heath . . .'

'Stop it, Sasha!' he commanded tautly. 'You'll do no such thing. Do I make myself very clear?' He sat up and again she felt the blue fire of his eyes scorching her. 'Do I, Sasha?' he repeated violently when she didn't speak.

She trembled inwardly, but her voice was surprisingly resolute. 'It's the other way around, Heath. I don't think I've made myself clear. Because you see, if you go, there's no way you can stop me from letting

Stephanie know the *whole* story, the neuro-surgeon's
. . . unease, everything. That would be a nice way to end
a honeymoon, wouldn't it?'

She closed her eyes and waited for the explosion she
was sure would come. Then when nothing happened,
she opened them to see him staring at her with his lips
tightly compressed and a nerve beating in his jaw. And
when he spoke finally, the contempt in his voice was
frightening.

'What a busy little bee you've been today, Sasha. Just
how the hell did you find out about this?'

She compressed her lips.

'Sasha!'

She looked away and he swore then so that she
flinched, but still she refused to speak.

'Well, I don't believe you'd do it to her,' he said
finally. 'Would you, Sasha? I mean what would be the
point once I was gone? Or hadn't you thought of that
one?' he asked with dangerous quiet that didn't fool her
for a moment.

'Just try me, Heath,' she said, looking at him
steadfastly. 'And *this* is the point. Your mother is now
my stepmother and we're a family now whether you like
it or not. And I have no doubt in my own mind that she
would do anything for me. Anything, Heath. So how do
you think I could ever face her again if I let you wander
off in this condition? And do you think she'd ever
forgive me if you did go and I said nothing? The point
is that simple, Heath, and so is the choice. Either you
stay here and put up with me, or you go, with the sure
knowledge that she'll be searching the world for you.'

The silence was intense as they stared at each other
like two bitter combatants locked in a mortal struggle.

Then Heath deliberately relaxed his expression,
although there was something strangely alert in his eyes
which puzzled her.

'Sasha,' he said speaking coolly and evenly, 'we once

decided that you had an adolescent crush on me. Don't you think you're confusing this . . . rash of concern and family feeling with some stray remnants of that?'

She moved then to cut off his words before they could inflict any more pain on her. She pushed her chair back and stood up, and in her heart, she thought, I hate you, Heath Townsend. I do. And before she could stop herself she found that spark of hatred speaking for her.

'You can think that if you like,' she said, matching his cool, even tones. 'But if that's what's bothering you, can I tell you something? Brent . . . well, he wants to marry me. Only he says he won't rush me into anything, although I . . . well, I don't see why we should wait. But anyway, when I told him about you, he seemed to think it would be good for me to be away from him for a while to make very sure of what I felt. Although,' she looked at Heath straightly, 'I don't think it will affect the final outcome. But I want to thank you, Heath, for . . . well,' she looked away and coloured, 'I was very silly that night—the night of the party—and you were very wise. And I really appreciate what you did now.'

Oh, what are you saying, Sasha? she asked herself as that spark of emotion and hatred died with her words, leaving her feeling drained and so cold. How could you?

She moved restlessly and turned away from the table towards the door. Then she made herself stop and turn back, to see him staring across the room away from her.

She waited for a moment, but he didn't stir.

'Heath?'

It seemed like an eternity before he moved his head, but only to look down at his glass, not at her.

'What is it?' he asked, sounding remote and uninterested.

'Please don't go, will you? I . . . meant what I said. Don't make me do it.'

She didn't wait for an answer.

CHAPTER SIX

THE first week passed agonisingly slowly.

Heath didn't mention the subject of his going or staying, but Sasha knew he would stay, although sometimes she hated herself for using such a strong lever against him. He also avoided her as much as possible and when it was unavoidable he was curt and brief with her. But she schooled herself to betray no reaction and set about making life as comfortable for him as she could.

It wasn't easy, because it was like living with a stranger, and added to this she had the problem of what she had said to him about Brent to worry about. Not only because she had spoken for Brent before he had spoken for himself—although that was bad enough, she mused one evening, breaking out into a sweat at the thought of her own temerity, but also because of the intrinsic lie she had told. Not that she doubted for one minute that she would have acted exactly the same way even if she had been head over heels in love with Brent. But another truth was, she wasn't head over heels in love with Brent, and for one very good reason.

'Yet if Heath thinks I had any hope of trying to make him fall in love with me,' she muttered spiritedly, 'well, I gave up that idea long ago. So there was no need to say those things to me and . . . goad me into lying to him. And if I'm doing it and I can't help loving him,' she went on rebelliously, 'that's a different matter. So put that in your pipe and smoke it, Heath Townsend!'

Then she sighed dismally and wondered if she really knew what she felt for Heath. And she began to worry again about Brent. Because she knew he would be out

79

to see her sooner or later. And something in his voice when she had spoken to him on the phone and explained why she was resigning so precipitously had made her feel very wary—particularly in the light of what she had said to Heath.

'Oh dear,' she murmured, 'what a mess!'

'What?'

She jumped and turned to see Heath standing in the doorway watching her. They had had their dinner in the usual strained atmosphere, which was beginning to cause Edith's face to twitch uncomfortably, and then Heath had retired to his study and firmly closed the door.

Sasha had come to sit in front of the fire and ponder her problems.

'Nothing!' she said hastily.

Heath regarded her thoughtfully for a moment and then limped forward to take the plump comfortable armchair opposite her.

'Could it be that you're beginning to regret having acted so high-handedly, sweet stepsister?' he asked mockingly.

She looked across at him in the firelight. 'You're not making it very easy for me,' she said reproachfully.

'What would you like me to do?' he said acidly. 'Let you hold my hand and bathe my brow?'

She grinned ruefully. 'I can't imagine it. But maybe I could read to you, or for you. Doctor James said you were experiencing some sort of visual distortions which must make it difficult,' she finished tentatively, but then added more stoutly, 'I'm a very good reader.'

'Says who?' he asked coolly.

'Says me! Didn't you know I was a bit of a genius in that line? Why, I've been known to lay 'em in the aisles!' She grimaced laughingly. 'I even won a medal at my last school Eisteddfod with my very moving rendition of *The Man from Snowy River*. Let's see— how does it go again . . .'

'Spare me, Sasha.' He held up a hand, but she thought she detected a gleam of amusement in his eyes as he added, 'Nobody could possibly remember it all anyway.'

'Want to bet? Nobody who had a mad English teacher like I had could possibly forget it. He used to break out into it at least twice a period. It's very stirring too. I mean, I really love Banjo Patterson's poetry,' she said seriously. 'Don't you?'

'Yes, but . . .'

'You're right.' She sighed theatrically but with her lips twitching. Then she sobered completely. 'But we could . . . talk, and listen to music, walk together and play cards or chess. And I could read the papers to you, keep you updated on world affairs.'

'I can listen to the radio for that,' he said after a moment, the amusement gone.

'Heath, please don't shut me out like this,' she said huskily. 'I feel bad enough as it is, but I had to do it.'

'And now you have to live with it,' he said quietly. 'Tell me, does Brent intend to shut himself off from you entirely during this period?'

'Oh no,' she said uncomfortably. 'He's coming out soon. But he's very busy at the moment. Do you mind?'

'Mind what?'

'Brent coming out here. You haven't been in touch with anyone so far.'

He looked into the fire and didn't speak.

'He's a very great friend of yours, Heath,' she said softly.

'What did you tell him?'

'I—just that you were home and not well and needed someone. And I made him promise not to tell anyone else. I know he won't.'

She waited with bated breath, but all he said eventually, in dry tones, was, 'I had no idea when I nicknamed you, Napoleon, just how apt it would be.'

And he stood up awkwardly and left the room without another word, leaving Sasha staring into the fire, conscience-stricken.

But the next morning two things happened to ease her conscience somewhat. Doctor James arrived while they were still at breakfast. Heath immediately cast Sasha a resigned, cynical look which the doctor intercepted.

'No, she didn't call me, Heath,' he said firmly. 'I came quite off my own bat. And just to set the record straight, if you've made other plans, I'll go. If not, I think we should come to some agreement. You need medical care, and I could begin it right now.' He eyed Heath with his no-nonsense look that Sasha vividly remembered from her own childhood.

And she saw Heath do battle with his own emotions and once more she waited with bated breath. But he stood up finally with a shrug yet tightened lips before he said, 'Lead on. I'm with you.'

After the examination Heath stayed in his room and Doctor James came to find Sasha. 'You're a good girl,' he said abruptly, 'but I'm not sure if you haven't bitten off more than you can chew.'

'Neither am I,' she said with a humourless smile. 'But I can keep trying. Just tell me what I must do.'

'Well, he's agreed to see another specialist, so I'll set up the appointment. So far as his leg goes, the muscles need exercise, which as you can see is painful. I'll arrange for a physiotherapist to treat him daily, which might mean driving him into Penrith. Walking, provided you don't let him overdo it, would be good for him.'

'This specialist is a neuro-surgeon?'

'Yes. A brilliant one too, and I'm hoping he'll consult with the first man Heath saw, who also has a considerable reputation in the field. So that they might track his exact progress—or lack of it—between them.'

'He never talks about his eyes—I mean, his sight.'

'His eyes are perfectly healthy, Sasha.' He hesitated. 'His state of mind bothers me somewhat, I must admit.'

'Me too. I sometimes wish I hadn't done what I did,' she said sombrely.

'I know what you mean. But then it's often not easy to tread the right road. And you must never forget what he's been through.'

'I wish he'd tell me!'

'He told me a little of it just now. Apparently he lay for nearly two days in some ghastly battlefield with a skirmish going on about him before he could be got out. It's a miracle he didn't die from loss of blood or infection.'

'Why didn't he let us know?' she sighed despairingly. 'Or his paper?'

'Because for a long time he didn't even know who he was himself, my dear. Nor did anyone else. Then, as he said to me, it seemed superfluous to worry you all unnecessarily. And he wasn't working for any particular news service, you see. He was there quite independently. I presume his mother is used to him sort of disappearing for long stretches of time?'

'You presume right,' Sasha said sadly. 'And for a journalist, he's a lousy correspondent. That's why she hated him going off so much, because she was liable not to hear from him for ages. But as she said often too, if you could pin Heath down ... well, he wouldn't be quite Heath, would he?'

The second surprise came later in the day. After lunch Sasha did a totally uncharacteristic thing. She sat down in front of the fire to warm herself and promptly fell asleep.

She awoke some two hours later to find Heath standing over her with a newspaper in his hand, and she sat up with a hand to her mouth and her grey eyes round and slightly perplexed as she struggled with the remnants of a deep sleep.

'Heath?' she said uncertainly, then it all came crowding back to her and for an instant the vulnerability showed clearly in her eyes as she waited and wondered how he would try to demolish her this time.

His face tightened momentarily, then he said unemotionally, 'Don't look so guilty, Sasha. Here,' he tossed the newspaper into her lap and sat down.

'You want me to read it to you?' she asked stupidly.

He moved his head impatiently and said irritably, 'I don't want you to paper the walls with it.'

So she read, at first hesitantly and almost shyly, and mentally castigating herself for her showing off last night. But he said nothing, just lay back in his chair with his eyes closed, until she gained confidence and launched into a very funny report about a woman who had found a snake in her laundry and spent the whole day sitting on top of her washing machine in consequence.

She burst out laughing.

'But the worst part—it was dead,' she said, still chuckling. 'Only she didn't realise it.'

'It might have died of fright,' he said with a faint grin tugging at his lips. 'Can you just picture a frantic lady leaping on to her washing machine with accompanying sound effects?'

Edith came in then with a tea tray and set it down between them. She didn't say anything, but as she left the room she winked at Sasha.

'Go on,' said Heath idly after she had poured the tea.

'What would you like?' she asked. 'The trials and tribulations of the government, or cricket?'

'How about racing?'

Sasha wrinkled her nose. 'Very boring.'

'On the contrary, I find it very interesting. In fact in

lieu of anything better to do, I might turn to a life of gambling.'

'You don't mean go to the races?' she asked wide-eyed.

'No. But I could open a telephone betting account.'

'Are you serious, Heath?' she demanded.

He looked thoughtful and then relented. 'No—at least not about that side of it. But between us, my dear mama and I have some valuable brood mares eating their heads off in the paddock which we've neglected lately. Come spring they should be got in foal so that they can pay for their keep so to speak.'

Sasha drew an excited breath. 'Do you mean we should . . . do a bit of research and pick out stallions to send them too?'

'It's just an idea,' he drawled. 'We could be too late. A lot of the top class stallions would have had their books closed by now.'

'Ah,' she said thoughtfully. 'A problem, I admit.'

'I didn't think you ever admitted that,' he said with a sudden flashing look of amusement that took her breath away because it reminded her so forcibly of the old Heath. And all her nerve endings seemed to come alive, and that old longing to reach over and touch him, so that she swallowed unexpectedly and looked away confusedly.

'What is it, Sasha?'

'Nothing,' she said hastily, and put down her cup. 'I . . . I was just thinking, we could try, couldn't we? I think your mother has every book on breeding that was ever published here, and we might even find some not so fashionable stallions yet, but with the right bloodlines to match the mares. Why we might even get a nick,' she said with genuine excitement, referring to that elusive matching of bloodlines that throws champions.

His blue eyes searched her face for a long time and

she waited anxiously with her heart beating that strange tattoo again.

Then he said, 'You're very sweet and you're very young, Sasha. I'm sorry I've been so harsh with you.' He looked suddenly tired as he added, 'If you want to go to all the trouble, I suppose it's as good a way as any of trying to while away the time.'

It was only that night in the privacy of her bedroom that Sasha allowed herself to wonder uncomfortably, if Heath hadn't seen right through her today. And she felt hot and cold by turns as she examined the strength of her feelings this afternoon, and how difficult it was going to be not to betray herself.

She lay in bed and listened to the wind surging round the old house and couldn't prevent herself from thinking of Heath lying not many rooms away from her. She caught her breath and felt a tremor shake her from head to toe as she pictured herself lying beside him, quietly, with her hands on his body soothing away the pain and the tension. Then the picture changed and she imagined his hands on her body, stroking her, and she knew a terrifying sense of desolation because it could never be.

The next few days passed peacefully.

Sasha got out all Stephanie's books on breeding and Heath went along with her enthusiasm in a strangely gentle mood that secretly tore at her heartstrings.

The weather warmed slightly and they went for a walk every afternoon down the paddock, Heath wearing old jeans and an older sheepskin coat and dark glasses to protect his eyes, and Sasha in an alpaca wool poncho that Stephanie and her father had sent from South America and a green woollen cap with a pom-pom.

It was slow progress, and most days she had to find a

place for him to rest for a few minutes before they made the return journey. And it was on one of these walks that she discovered that the truce—if that was what it was—between them was a very precarious thing.

Heath was more silent than usual and when she put her hand through his arm as they came to a rough patch of ground she felt him tense distinctly even through the thickness of his coat. She took her hand away immediately and tried to think of something to say.

Unfortunately, in her concern, she tripped over a hidden rock herself and instinctively clutched at the first thing that came to hand. Which happened to be Heath.

She heard him take a sharp breath as he put his full weight on his bad leg and she sprang away, but it was too late. His face went white with pain and he swayed where he stood and would have fallen if she hadn't reached out again this time to steady him and take his weight on her.

'I'm so sorry,' she gasped. 'Are you all right?'

'Yes,' he said tightly.

'Won't you sit down? There's a boulder just behind you.'

'No! I'm fine. So you can stop clutching me like a mother hen,' he said shortly.

Sasha took a step backwards experimentally and saw the effort it was costing him to stand upright. 'Heath, don't be silly,' she pleaded with her hands on his arms.

'Get *away* from me, Sasha,' he ground out.

'B-but . . .' she faltered.

'Just do it,' he said violently. Then he closed his eyes briefly. 'It's got to come some time,' he added in more normal tones. 'I can't use you as a crutch for the rest of my life.'

'Well, I know that,' she said shakily, 'only . . .'

'You don't know anything about it,' he said shortly, 'or you wouldn't be here forcing these attentions on me that I don't want. Take your hand away, Sasha,' he commanded curtly.

She stared up into the navy blue of his eyes and knew that she would be in tears in a moment. She took her hand away quickly and turned so that he couldn't see her face.

'Oh, for Pete's sake. let's go home,' he said impatiently.

'So they did, and all the while Sasha told herself to ignore his taunts, but it was easier said than done and the bright, cold afternoon turned inexplicably dark for her.

Dinner was strained again that evening, so that Edith's long nose quivered as she sensed it like a bloodhound, but she said nothing, not even to Sasha when they were alone with Heath's study door firmly closed against them.

He'll come round in the morning, Sasha told herself dismally as she chose to go to bed rather than face a long empty evening.

But she couldn't sleep and she couldn't get anything she wanted to listen to on her bedside radio, nor did she have anything to read, so she finally gave up the struggle and slipped her blue velvet dressing gown on and matching slippers, and crept into the lounge to stoke up the fire. The house was in darkness and quite silent, so she assumed Heath must have gone to bed. She made herself a cup of cocoa and took it back to the fire, but found she had trouble sitting still, so she roamed restlessly around the room and finally stopped in front of the record player to flip idly through the dozens of records Heath and his mother owned.

'Isn't it a good night for Gilbert and Sullivan?' Heath asked broodingly from across the room just as she turned away impatiently.

She didn't jump, and wondered if despair had affected her reflexes as well. He was still dressed but with his dark, gold-streaked hair ruffled.

'No.'

'Oh?' he said, and limped into the room. 'Don't tell me our very model of a modern major-general has decided to . . . quit?'

She didn't answer and stood quite still as he came right up to her and put his hand out to touch the long swathe of auburn hair that lay across one shoulder.

'What would it take to make you quit, Sasha?' he asked very quietly. She lifted her eyes, expecting to see them hard and mocking, but there was just a genuine enquiry in their dark blue depths and the skin beneath looked bruised against his pallor as if he had spent too many a sleepless night.

'I told you,' she whispered.

'You're a very stubborn child,' he commented at last as he leant his shoulders back against the wall, his fingers still fiddling with her hair.

'I'm not a child any more, Heath,' she said quietly. 'Maybe I was . . . before, but I've grown up in these last six months.' She tilted her chin upwards. 'Maybe that's why I won't quit,' she said barely audibly.

Something sharpened in his eyes, something she didn't understand.

'How have you grown up, Sasha?'

She shrugged faintly. 'Lots of ways, I suppose. I can't show it to you in inches, it wasn't that kind of growing, but . . .'

'Maybe it was this kind, then,' he said, and brought his other hand up to slip it round her waist and spread his fingers over the small of her back to draw her against him.

She felt his breath fan her forehead and her eyes widened incredulously as his other hand left her hair and slid round her shoulders to pull her even closer so she was lying against him in his arms, pressed to his body.

'This way,' he said again, against the corner of her mouth. 'Kiss me, Sasha.'

She moved then as a small explosion of panic took hold of her, but Heath's arms were unrelenting . . . No, she thought dimly, not that, they just make me feel as if I fit here, as if I was moulded to melt into Heath's body and nowhere else. But . . .

'Heath, *no*!' she protested breathlessly as he lowered his head to kiss the delicate area of her throat, so that her skin shivered of its own accord.

'No?' he said at last, raising his head to send her a pure blue gaze from beneath half-lowered lids. 'It was a little different last time, wasn't it? Then it was—kiss me, please, Heath. And, don't stop, please—don't torment me like this, Heath.'

She flushed brilliantly. 'I . . .'

'You what, Sasha?' he said, his lips barely moving.

'I . . . I'm—oh, Heath, let me go!'

'Why should I?' he said sombrely. 'Do you know how long it is since I had a woman? Don't you know you shouldn't go wandering around in the depth of the night in your nightgown with your hair loose?

A spark of indignation lit her eyes. 'I wasn't looking for this! You make it sound as if . . . I'm quite well dressed, as it happens.'

'Are you?' he questioned with a faint smile curving his lips. His hold slackened and he pushed her away from him and repositioned his hands so that he was holding her beneath the armpits. 'Why, Sasha,' he said feigning surprise, 'I don't believe you're wearing a bra!'

She stared up at him, her lips parted disbelievingly as his hands moved and then as if impatient with the layers of velvet and fine Viyella, moved again, expertly, to loosen the sash of her dressing gown so that it fell open, and then with a flick of his fingers, the buttons of her nightgown gave way and his hands were sliding beneath it.

It was like an electric shock, the feel of his strong fingers on her breasts, stroking, cupping, teasing her nipples until they stood erect, two hardening peaks she couldn't deny even if she had wanted to.

'Heath,' she said despairingly in her throat.

But he ignored her plea and opened her nightgown further to free her breasts and lay his lips on them, while she thought she might faint with the exquisite pleasure of what he was doing to her.

Then suddenly she was at arm's length and Heath was looking down at her with all the cynicism she had ever seen in his eyes. 'I told you once it was all there in good ... working order,' he said, his eyes glinting strangely. 'And you were very cross with me at the time, sweetheart, if I recall. But I don't suppose this is such virgin territory now.' His hands moved in on her again.

'*Don't!*' she cried involuntarily, not to his hands but his words and the look in his eyes as they rested indifferently on her hot face.

There was a tiny silence. Then Heath said cruelly, 'You should have slapped my face long ago, Sasha.'

She recoiled as if it was she who had received a blow as the implication of his words sank in. 'I should,' she said torturedly. 'And I would if you weren't ... if you weren't ...' She stopped abruptly and sucked in a scared breath at the look of menace on his face.

'Do you have to keep reminding me of it, Sasha?' he said violently, and almost threw her from him so that she stumbled and tears of anger and humiliation beaded her lashes as she regained her balance and with shaking fingers pulled her nightgown together and re-tied the sash of her robe.

He had turned away from her, but he swung back now with an impatient curse beneath his breath and pulled her back into his arms.

'I'm *sorry*,' he said into her hair. 'Don't look like that.'

It was some moments before the tremors that shook her subsided.

'That's better,' said Heath at last, and drew away. 'I'm going to bed. Stay here and play some music if you want to.'

She nodded, unable to speak, as she fingered her sash.

'Sasha?'

She lifted her eyes at last.

Heath bit his lip. 'Nothing,' he said. 'Goodnight, Blossom.' He limped out.

CHAPTER SEVEN

It was Edith, the next morning, who brought a strange kind of logic to Heath's actions of the previous day.

At breakfast Heath said casually, 'By the way, I forgot to tell you, Sasha, Brent rang up yesterday and I invited him out for lunch. Edith's going to drive me into Penrith this morning, so you'll have the place to yourselves until we get back. He said he'd be here by about ten.' He stood up and reached for his cane. 'I'll be ready in an hour, Edith.'

'Will you be back for lunch?' Sasha asked, feeling suddenly numb with fright.

'Brent seemed to think it would be a good idea, but we could always have lunch in Penrith, if you preferred, couldn't we, Edith?' he said, casting that good lady an amused look.

Edith's nose twitched and she tucked her lips primly together. She'd never known how to handle Heath and after the trauma of their week alone together had secretly been only too relieved to close off her channel of communication with him and leave it to Sasha. In fact if it wasn't for her feelings for Stephanie, Sasha often thought Edith would class Heath as the devil's representative himself!

And the thought of them sharing lunch together brought an involuntary smile to Sasha's face despite her other problems.

'Oh . . . no!' she exclaimed.

He looked at her thoughtfully for a minute, then shrugged and turned to leave.

Edith got up and closed the door behind him. 'I know what's biting him,' she said grimly as she poured them each another cup of coffee.

Sasha blinked. 'You do?'

'Yes. That woman again.' Edith's tones conveyed a power of contempt.

'Which—do you mean Veronica?' queried Sasha incredulously.

Edith snorted in agreement.

'But how?' Sasha asked stupidly. 'He hasn't seen anyone.'

'Well, he'll be seeing her shortly, mark my words. According to your Brent,' Sasha had brought Brent out one Sunday a couple of months ago and he'd made quite a hit with Edith, 'she's heard a rumour that Heath's back in the country, and what's more, she's hot on the trail. Hot to trot, as they say,' she added, so uncharacteristically that Sasha had to smile again.

Then her smile faded. 'But how do you know all this, Edith?' she queried.

Edith looked a shade uncomfortable. Then she said forthrightly, 'When Mr Havelock rang yesterday I picked up the kitchen extension at the same time as Heath lifted the study one.' She sniffed. 'I didn't mean to go on listening, but—oh well, I suppose I couldn't resist it. He—your Brent told Heath that *Miss* Gardiner had been on to him saying she'd heard a rumour that Heath was back in town.'

Of course, Sasha thought dazedly. That explains it! He still loves Veronica, but he doesn't want to tie her down to . . . to someone who might be going blind. No wonder he was so tense yesterday and so—well, like he was last night. Because I'm the one keeping him here for her to find, and making his frustration so much worse. Oh, heavens, she thought, genuinely appalled, What have I done?

'. . . Sasha?'

Sasha came back from her thoughts with a start. 'Sorry I was miles away,' she said to Edith's look of enquiry.

Edith looked at her with narrowed eyes for a time. Then she said, 'I was only telling you not to worry about lunch. I've made something up that only needs heating when I get back. So you go ahead and enjoy yourself this morning, Blossom. You deserve it!' she added militantly.

I don't know what I deserve, Sasha thought as she watched Brent's car pull up on the gravel, but perhaps I ought to have my head read . . .

'So tell me about Heath,' said Brent when they were sitting in the lounge.

He had greeted her so affectionately and there had been so much news for him to tell her about the television series, now actually in the filming stage, that they had found themselves walking around the garden in their enthusiasm for a good half hour before she had laughingly invited him inside and offered him a beer.

She looked across at him affectionately, this tall, ruggedly strong man who could be so gentle and understanding and such a good friend, and sighed.

'What is it?' he asked intently.

'Oh, Brent—well, you'll see for yourself,' she answered unhappily. 'But I'm afraid I've made an awful mess of things on top of it.'

'Tell me,' he said quietly, and for a minute her heart went out almost in love to him and she wondered miserably why she couldn't make it the real thing.

She told him nearly everything. About the threat that was hanging over Heath's head, how she'd stopped him from leaving the country, how Edith had overheard their telephone conversation yesterday and how Heath had reacted—a part of it, anyway.

When she'd finished Brent put his glass down and said, 'It's true. Veronica rang me and said she'd heard he was back. She begged me to tell her if I knew anything more. I told her I didn't and I really hoped I put her off the scent. But then when I spoke to Heath yesterday, I realised she was just as liable to come out here one day and maybe he'd like to be ... fore-warned. 'But,' he looked at her searchingly, 'he took it very calmly, Sasha. As if he really didn't care one way or the other.'

'I'm sure he does,' she said. 'You weren't in the country when they were together, were you? And you didn't see him that night after ... after I did my little act. Then there's the way he was yesterday—I'm *sure* he hasn't got over her, Brent. I just don't know why I didn't think of it before.'

They sat in silence for a few minutes and then Sasha drew a deep breath and said, 'There's something else I have to tell you. I ... when I first saw how he was and decided to do what I did, I concocted an excuse on the spur of the moment for resigning from my work with you.' She stopped and then said awkwardly, 'It was a bit silly, but I was hard pressed and I didn't want him to have it on his conscience—you know, ruining my career and so on. I told him you wanted to marry me but you thought I needed time away from you to ... to think about it,' she finished lamely, and felt herself go scarlet at the same time.

But she met his gaze steadfastly and flinched at the wonder in his eyes.

'It was all I could think of,' she said when he didn't speak. 'I'm sorry ...'

'Don't be sorry, Sasha. You see, you read my mind perfectly. I do want to marry you. And the only reason I didn't come out here the day you resigned, rather forcibly stopped myself from coming,' he added with a wry grin, 'was because I told myself I shouldn't rush you. That maybe I was going too fast for you. So you told him nothing but the truth, Sasha.'

She stared at him and was suddenly almost overwhelmed by a desire to tell him the whole truth, but she knew she couldn't. She dropped her eyes in confusion and started as he reached over and took one of her hands in his.

'There's something else, isn't there, Sasha?' he said quietly.

'N-no,' she whispered.

'But there is,' he said quietly. 'And I must tell you I know what it is, because I can't bear to see you looking like this. You fell in love with Heath, didn't you, Sasha? Perhaps a long time ago?'

Her lashes flew upwards. 'You know?' she gasped incredulously.

'I think I knew from that first day we met by accident in town,' Brent said gently.

'And ... and you still want to marry me?' she stammered.

'Yes. The fact that you love Heath doesn't seem to make me stop loving you, you see,' he said gravely.

'But what if I never stop loving Heath?' she said, suddenly agitated. 'Do you know, I've jumped on this feeling I have for him and I've kicked it around and I've ... pretended to myself it's only what half the women in Australia felt for him and I've tried to accept ... other people's views that it's something I'll grow out of,' she said bitterly, 'but . . .'

'Heath's view, you mean?' he interrupted acutely.

'Yes,' she said desolately after a moment. 'I don't understand why you want to marry me, because I've got this awful feeling I won't change!'

'I wouldn't be asking you to,' he said with compassion. 'But if Heath doesn't feel the way you do, while it might always be there, it must fade somewhat, and one day you might wake up and discover you have room in your heart for another love.'

She looked at him uncertainly.

'Sasha, it happens to so many people.'

'Has it happened to you?' she asked.

'In a way. I thought I'd washed my hands of it for ever. Then one day I met you.'

'Now I really feel terrible,' she said weakly, and was surprised to see him smile at her with genuine amusement.

'You mustn't,' he said. 'These are the things you can't change. You can't help being Sasha Derwent who strayed across Brent Havelock's path any more than . . .'

'Heath can help being Heath Townsend who strayed across my path,' she finished for him, and found herself smiling through her tears. She pulled out her hanky and blew her nose. 'But can I say this? If it wasn't for Heath, and I sometimes wish *that* with all my heart, I'd have had no trouble falling in love with you. I mean . . . I didn't mean to say that.' She stopped in intolerable confusion. 'It's just . . . I wasn't *comparing* you.'

'I know what you mean. Love isn't a measuring game. We fall for who we fall for, and not necessarily the best person for us. Like . . . Veronica perhaps, but then who are we to say? Just do one thing for me, Sasha? Remember what I've said because I meant it with all my heart. And in the meantime, don't worry that I'll give you away unless for some reason you ever want me to.'

She lifted his hand and pressed it to her cheek. 'I won't forget,' she promised. 'And thank you.'

They stayed like that for a few moments. Then the door swung open and Heath stood there. His face was paper-white against the deep blue pools of his eyes and Sasha wanted to run to him because he looked so tired and sick. But she stopped herself after the involuntary tensing of her limbs and Brent's fingers moved on her cheek for a second. Then he dropped his hand away and stood up.

'Heath—Oh, it's good to see you, mate,' he said, his voice low but intense with feeling.

A strange expression crossed Heath's face, a mixture of infinite weariness and something Sasha couldn't name, and she found she was holding her breath, but she didn't know why.

Then he moved his shoulders and said quietly, 'It's good to see you, Brent. You might never know how good, friend.' There was an unmistakable depth of meaning in his voice that touched Sasha, and she felt as if the burden round her heart was lightened a little by this exchange of feeling between the two men who, apart from her father, she admired most in the world.

Edith bustled in laden with parcels to break up the moment, and she made a big fuss of Brent, which caused Heath to raise his eyebrows sardonically. Then and a few more times during lunch. But whatever his thoughts on the subject were he didn't express them.

In fact the meal turned out to be a whole lot easier than Sasha had dared to hope, and Heath even went so far as to talk about some of his experiences in response to Brent's questioning, the first time he had done so, although he had refused to be drawn on the fact that he had been wounded, beyond a glinting smile and the same thing he had said to Sasha—I ran out of luck . . .

But after lunch when they were sitting on the verandah making the best of some wintry sunshine and the strange beauty of the naked landscape beyond the garden fence, he said suddenly, 'Sasha tells me my favourite kid . . . stepsister and one of my best friends have fallen in love.'

He turned his head towards Brent, but his eyes were masked by his dark glasses.

Sasha froze, but Brent took his time in answering. He said finally 'Your kid sister is one of the most beautiful, nicest young women I've met. Do you mind?' he added abruptly.

Sasha became aware of Heath's fingers drumming on the wicker arm of his chair.

He said, 'It isn't up to me to mind, so much. But Sasha takes her family responsibilities very seriously, I've discovered, which led me to think I should too. And if it was anyone else I'd say—as I said to her once before—wait, take your time. But now that it's you, Brent, and I've seen you two together—well, I only want to say that it's what is in your hearts that counts. Not some advice from me or anyone else.'

Brent stared out over the garden. 'If Sasha wants to wait, that's all right with me. You mentioned that she takes her family responsibility very seriously. I don't mind that, because it's all part of Sasha—she takes all her responsibilities seriously. And with love and sensitivity. If she felt less for you, when you needed someone, it would mean she felt less for me ultimately. And I think I'm too old to say to someone, all that feeling must be directed only at *me*, because then one day it might mean I was jealous of my own children because Sasha loved them. Do you see? So if she wants to wait, we'll wait.'

Heath moved restlessly and Sasha had the strangest feeling that they were discussing something she wasn't privy to. As if there were some unspoken truths flowing between them.

Then he said, 'Don't wait too long, will you? With the best of intentions, let alone the worst, some things seem to slip away from you before you're fully aware of what they mean.'

He must have meant Veronica, Sasha thought later, much later when she was leaning out of her bedroom window despite the dark, frosty air.

She watched her breath hang suspended in a white cloud. Then the moon came out and the beauty of it shining starkly on the garden and the paddock beyond caught at her throat and brought tears to her eyes. Tears that had been lurking in her heart ever since she had sat and listened to Heath urge her and Brent to get married. And with the tears came, she found, a curious feeling of resentment which led her to question again exactly what it was she felt for Heath Townsend. Perhaps love? Or perhaps it's just become a habit to think I love him, she mused. But anyway, if you still cherished a seed of hope that he would one day turn to you, Sasha, what happened today couldn't have killed it more effectively, could it?

Life settled back into its routine after Brent's visit. She drove Heath into town for physiotherapy most days and he had a consultation with the two neuro-surgeons. But she heistated to ask for the prognosis because he consistently refused to discuss his sight in any way with her, and because he came away from it looking wan and morose.

But she finally plucked up the courage as she carefully drove home.

'What did they say?' she asked.

'Not a great deal.'

'. . . Will they have to operate?'

'They don't know yet.'

'Maybe that's a good sign,' she said quietly.

'The only thing that would be good, Sasha,' he said savagely, 'would be not to have to sit through any more cautious dissertations on the subject of my sight, with you as well . . .'

But there was one source of satisfaction for her in that he was undeniably beginning to look better, more like the old Heath. And as his leg got stronger he began to take an interest in the running of the two properties, although this was not entirely pleasing to Edith, unfortunately.

But she saw the wisdom of not letting her emotions run away with her when Sasha pointed out that they were all the better off if Heath didn't have time hanging too hcavily on his hands.

And to Sasha's surprise, she realised one day that a month had passed since she had left town.

But despite the comparative peace and companionship they shared, she also realised there was an air of expectancy that they all shared too. Heath didn't show it outwardly, but Sasha knew it was there. She felt it in his sudden restless movements that he forcibly stilled.

And she knew immediately what Edith meant when she said one day out of the blue, 'I feel as if I'm living on a volcano!' but didn't elucidate.

For herself, she found that each night when she got into bed, she sent up a little prayer of thanks that it hadn't happened, although she couldn't understand why it hadn't happened. She would have loved to be able to discuss it with Brent, but he was away in the Northern Territory filming.

It was quite by chance that she discovered why Veronica hadn't contacted Heath. She was paging through a woman's magazine one evening when her eyes fell on the shimmering blonde hair that was so distinctively Veronica's, and those beautiful features and sinuous figure. She read the caption to the picture. Veronica Gardiner, it said, one of the brightest lights of radio and television, had recently left Sydney for a three-week stint in the South Pacific as co-ordinator of a new series of television programmes on holidays in that area. As well as directing the series she would be taking part in it as commentator in several of the resorts and areas the programme would detail. What a nice way to combine work and pleasure! the caption finished impudently.

Sasha let the magazine fall into her lap as she stared across the room unseeingly. So that was why she hadn't come! But she was only going to be away for three weeks, according to the magazine, and two of those weeks could have already passed if she had left soon after contacting Brent . . .

But whenever she gets back, Sasha thought, isn't she bound to try and find Heath? Unless Brent managed to convince her he wasn't in Australia?

She shivered suddenly and the magazine slid to the floor. She bent forward to retrieve it and noticed that Heath was watching her from where he was lounging on the settee. She felt herself colour, then deliberately relaxed her movements and tossed the magazine face downwards on to the table beside her.

Then she stood up and stretched and said teasingly, 'Heavens! It's only eight o'clock and I feel as if I could fall asleep. What shall we do?'

He raised his eyebrows. 'Go into town, take in a show, go on to a disco.'

She stared at him. 'Would you like to do that?'

'What do you think?' he said caustically.

'I don't know,' she said after a moment. 'I mean, I don't know if that's what you'd like to do if you could, or . . .' She hesitated.

'Or what? Never mind,' he said impatiently after waiting for her to speak. 'The point is, because *I* can't, even if I wanted to, there's no reason for you to abstain totally. Why don't you take a few days off and do just that? Edith will look after me,' he added sourly, 'in case you're worried that I might nip off.'

Sasha sighed with exasperation. 'You're deliberately twisting my words, you know. I hadn't even thought of any of those things. *You* were the one.'

'But you're bored, aren't you?' Heath shot her a searching look.

Bored? she thought. On no. In a way I've never been more contented in my life. Which is where the danger lies, Sasha, so you'd better not get too used to it . . .

'Are you trying to concoct some lies to tell me, Sasha?' he asked, breaking in on her thoughts. 'Some soft, suitable words to soothe the invalid with? Because you needn't bother,' he added dryly.

For some reason his words caused something to snap within her. So that she said acidly, 'What would be the use? If you're determined to feel so sorry for yourself— go ahead. As a matter of fact I think I'd enjoy to have a good fight with you right now, rather than soothe you in any way. Because I think you're impossible, Heath Townsend!'

She tilted her chin mutinously and then gasped as he sat up and shot out a hand to grasp her wrist and pull her down on to the settee beside him.

'All right, Napoleon,' he said, his eyes gleaming with devilry, 'now you're down to my level, go ahead.' He formed one of her hands into a fist and added, 'But I should warn you, I'm a lot stronger than I look.'

'Oh!' she breathed, now thoroughly incensed, 'you know I didn't mean that kind of a fight. But if you ever call me that again I will hit you! And if you must know, I'm sick to death of you patronising me! You do it all the time!'

'No, I don't,' he countered, with a smile tugging at the corners of his lips and his hand still around her clenched fist. 'In fact I thought I'd been very nice to you lately. I've been trying hard enough.'

'Well, that's just what I mean,' she spat at him. 'If that's not patronising me, I don't know what is!' She tried uselessly to pull her hand away.

Heath looked at her quizzically. 'Do you mean you'd rather I wasn't nice to you?' he asked gravely but with inner amusement.

'Yes! No. I mean . . . oh! You know exactly what I mean,' she said furiously. 'So you can just stop it! And while you're doing that, why don't you stop feeling so sorry for yourself too? It's . . .'

But she didn't get to finish what she was saying, because with a blaze of anger in his eyes, he jerked her into his arms and brought his mouth punishingly down on hers.

She tried to fight him, but it was a losing battle right from the start, and each attempt she made only seemed to spur him on until she went limp in his arms and he lifted his head at last to survey her frightened eyes and trembling, swollen lips with a curious look of torture in his own.

'Why . . . why did you do that?' she whispered at last, still lying in his arms and seemingly without the strength to move.

'Why? I don't know why,' he said after a moment, his voice strangely husky. He closed his eyes briefly and added, 'It's a good way to stop an argument, I guess, although I didn't mean to be so brutal. But perhaps you touched a nerve, Sasha. Only if I do feel sorry for myself, I . . . sometimes can't help thinking I have good cause. One that you wouldn't understand, though,' he added, and with an achingly familiar gesture gently tucked a wayward strand of hair behind her ear.

'Why don't you try me?' she murmured.

They stared at each other and then she felt him shrug slightly. 'I've got a better idea. Why don't I kiss you again?' he said, his lips barely moving, 'so that I can know I didn't do any lasting damage for Brent to have to cope with.'

Sasha's grey eyes were like deep pools in the pale perfect oval of her face.

'Is it . . . like falling off a horse?' she asked uncertainly after a small eternity.

His arms moved about her and he smiled down at her, a smile that she had seen before, as if it hurt him. 'You're so sweet, Sasha,' he said very quietly. 'Yes, I guess it could become that way, so try and forget it if you can.' He loosened his arms and sat her up in the corner of the settee, then rested his lips just lightly on hers for a moment before he stood up.

She put a hand to her mouth and looked up at him helplessly.

'I'm sure Brent can eradicate the memory of it, on second thoughts,' Heath said evenly. And then with a faint grin, 'If I say I'm tired and wouldn't mind going to bed, do you think you'd let me go without worrying whether I was feeling sorry for myself?' he asked.

Sasha stayed for a long time just staring into the fire. But when she finally decided to go to bed herself she noticed the light seeping from beneath his study door and winced.

And the next morning she tried to write her regular letter to Stephanie and her father, but after two attempts, tore it up dispiritedly, and it took a great effort to concentrate on anything else, she discovered.

CHAPTER EIGHT

'EDITH,' Sasha sighed helplessly, 'why did we start this?'

They stared at each other over an ever-growing assortment of clothes and miscellaneous objects that could perhaps be only kindly described as junk.

Edith's lips twitched and then they both burst out laughing. 'I'm sure I don't know, Sasha,' Edith said at last as she wiped her eyes. 'It seemed like a good idea at the time, but I had no idea Stephanie was such a hoarder!' She looked around at the spare bedroom which they'd chosen as their headquarters for their orgy of going though every cupboard and nook and cranny of the old house in a mistimed spring-cleaning attempt.

Edith queried with a look of wonder in her eyes as she scanned the room, 'Do you think she hired a ten-ton truck to bring it all here? I mean, she's only been here for a few years, she couldn't possibly have accumulated all this in that time.'

'Perhaps she did!' Sasha mused. 'Perhaps she'll hate us for throwing any of it out, what's more.'

'Pet, have you got room for all this at home?'

'Heavens, no!' said Sasha with a grin.

'Well then,' said Edith with a renewal of her zeal, 'we'll get rid of it. I managed to get hold of some tea chests and a lot of it can go to the Salvation Army. Although what even they'd do with something like this,' she looked down at a moth-eaten toy koala bear with both its eyes missing and one ear gone too, 'beats me!'

'Perhaps it was Heath's when he was a baby,' suggested Sasha with an impish grin. 'Actually it might be an idea . . .'

'I know,' Edith interrupted, 'not to throw anything of

Heath's away.' She grimaced and resignedly placed the bear on a pile of things to keep. 'Talking of Himself,' she added in the special tone of voice she reserved for dealing with this awkward subject, 'am I imagining things, or is he getting a little easier to live with?'

Sasha thought back to a certain episode which had taken place just two nights earlier and involuntarily her fingers went to her lips. But she said, 'I think he's making a real effort. Don't you think so, Edith?'

'Hmm.' Edith compressed her lips. 'It's all relative, I suppose. I mean, Heath as nice as pie can sometimes be as worrisome as Heath being his usual difficult self.' She stopped and smiled. 'That doesn't make much sense, I suppose, but do you know what I mean?'

'Got you!' Sasha said with an answering grin, then she sobered. 'Edith, do you think I should let anyone . . . know?' Sasha looked at the older woman with some of the turmoil she was going through etched plainly in her grey eyes.

'Stephanie?' Edith asked quickly.

'No,' Sasha said hesitantly. 'He'd be so angry if I did that, I don't think he'd ever forgive me. But I thought maybe . . . Veronica?'

They stared at each other over the pile of junk between them.

Then Edith said slowly, 'If you ask me, she'd run like a scalded cat rather than spend the rest of her life with a blind man.'

'But we don't *know* that,' Sasha said urgently. 'We don't know that he'll be blind and we don't know how she'd react. And after all, whatever we think of her, they were so very close once, weren't they? Maybe she could help him through this much better than I could.'

Edith picked up the koala bear again and regarded it thoughtfully. 'I doubt that,' she said at last. 'I don't think anyone could do that,' she added almost to herself, and went on rather hastily as a small frown gathered on Sasha's forehead, 'Sasha, I think we've done all we can do. We've sort of played God with Heath as it is. I think we should just leave things as they are now. Besides, she went on before Sasha could answer, 'all Veronica has to do is pick up a phone or drive out here to verify that rumour she heard. And all Heath has to do is pick up a phone if he wants her,' she added gently.

Sasha bit her lip. 'But don't you see, that's why he hasn't! He wouldn't inflict a blind man on her. And I think that's why he so much resented ... what I did. Because it meant it kept him within her reach.'

'I wonder,' Edith murmured. 'You're painting a very noble Heath.' She stared down at the koala bear unseeingly. 'But then perhaps you're right,' she said with a shrug.

'I'm pretty sure of it. And Veronica's out of the country now.'

'I know, I know, but she'll be back,' Edith muttered impatiently, but Sasha got the odd feeling that Edith's impatience was directed elsewhere, in fact it flashed across her mind that they were talking at cross-purposes.

'Look, leave it, Sasha,' said Edith as if taking a grip on herself. If you're right, he'll resent it very bitterly. And as I said, for Veronica, all it would take ... but there, I'm repeating myself. And you did the right thing, the only thing, Sasha,' she added reassuringly.

If only I were as sure of that, Sasha thought later when she and Heath were walking back to the house after a late afternoon stroll down to the river.

For a change it was a clear, gentle afternoon that seemed to match Heath's mood. There was no question of her having to help him any more, for although he still walked with a cane his leg was much stronger.

'How's the spring-cleaning going?' he asked lightly.

Sasha consciously packed away her more gloomy thoughts. 'Do you really want to know?' she asked with a grin.

'I see. I thought as much,' he said amusedly. 'Never mind, our Edith will see it through come hell or high water. It might keep her too occupied to meddle in my affairs for a day or two, for which the Lord be praised,' he added wryly, and looked at Sasha with his eyebrows raised, as she stopped walking and burst out laughing. 'What is it?' he asked.

'Just you . . . and Edith,' she said, still grinning. 'You do dislike each other so thoroughly, don't you?'

'Do we? I suppose we do. I'm not sure who started it, though. I first met her during my university days, in fact the very first time I met her, she pursed her lips primly at me as if I was Don Juan personified. And from then I . . . well . . .'

'You went out of your way to consolidate that impression?' Sasha teased.

Heath laughed ruefully. 'Perhaps I did,' he conceded. 'Anyway, it's been like a private war ever since. Who knows, though—we might end up very fond of each other one day! Beloved enemies. Stranger things have happened.'

'I think you might be that already,' said Sasha. 'Fond enemies. I'm sure Edith would miss it if she didn't have you to grumble about and vice versa.'

'Heaven forbid,' he said feelingly. 'But no, I have to admit I admire her tenacity. You two have a lot in common,' he added with a wicked little smile.

'Do we?' Sasha said innocently. 'I can't see it.'

'Only because basically you're shortsighted, Blossom, despite your claim to me once of being able to see from here to Bondi.'

'Not from here,' she protested.

'But you know what I mean, don't you, Sasha?' he said, and put an affectionate arm around her. 'Speaking as one shortsighted person to another. You literally and me potentially,' he added with a grimace.

'You make us sound like the blind leading the blind!' she teased with a smile, then she tensed and thought, why did I say that!

But Heath only pulled her a bit closer and she heard him laugh beneath his breath, so she relaxed and they moved on, hand in hand, not speaking, but on Sasha's part anyway, feeling so close to him she wondered if her heart might burst with foolish happiness.

Then they came within sight of the house, and Sasha stared and stumbled as she saw the strange car parked on the gravel and took in the person sitting on the verandah.

'What is it?' asked Heath immediately, and followed her gaze.

'I . . . I think it's Veronica,' she said, and fought to make her voice sound calm.

He swore.

For the first time in her life Veronica Gardiner seemed to be struck speechless as Sasha and Heath mounted the front steps. She got up slowly from her chair and the fingers that clutched her purse were white and her hazel eyes inexplicably wary as they never left Heath's face.

He asked abruptly, 'How are you, Veronica?'

She licked her lips. 'I'm fine, Heath. How are you? And you, Sasha?' She moved then as if to appear more normal. 'I didn't expect to see you here. I thought you'd be away filming with Brent. For that matter, I'm surprised to see you, Heath.'

'Are you?' he said a little dryly, and Sasha noted that of the three of them he seemed the least ill at ease, and she wondered what kind of iron control he was exercising, but there was nothing about him to give him away.

And Sasha knew suddenly what she had to do. She

said, 'Won't you have dinner with us, Veronica? It's a long drive.'

'I . . . thank you,' said Veronica. 'I'd like to.' But she looked a little uncertainly at Heath.

'Well, let's go in,' Sasha said brightly. 'It's getting cold out here. Does Edith know you're here?'

'Yes. I said I'd wait on the verandah for you.'

'Oh, good. Well, she'll probably be prepared, then. Let me take your coat,' she added briskly as she led the way into the lounge.

Veronica shed her coat obediently and stood in the middle of the room in a bewitching dress of lilac crêpe that moulded her superb figure and set off her fair hair perfectly.

Heath hadn't spoken, and beyond casting Sasha a strange look which she hadn't been able to interpret, he hadn't indicated whether he was pleased or not with this turn of events.

Now he said almost easily, 'Would you like a drink, Veronica? Sasha?'

Sasha saw Veronica relax visibly and said swiftly, 'You and Vernoica have one. I'll just go and see if Edith needs a hand. I won't be long.'

And she left the room with her heart beating erratically and her palms moist.

Edith was wearing her most constrained expression as she slammed a lid on a pot just as Sasha entered the kitchen.

'Sh-she's here,' Sasha said unnecessarily.

'I know that,' Edith replied.

'I guess you do. Did she say anything to you?'

Edith shrugged. 'She tried to pump me about Heath.'

'What did you say?' Sasha asked patiently, knowing Edith well in this mood.

'I said Heath never liked other people answering for him, so she'd better ask him herself.'

'Oh. I . . . asked her to stay to dinner.'

'I knew you'd do that,' Edith said resignedly. 'It'll be ready in half an hour.'

She sounded so cross that Sasha asked tentatively, 'Will you be having dinner with us? I wish I could think of a way we could let them eat on their own.'

'Well, there isn't,' Edith said forthrightly, 'so stop bothering about it. And I'll be there. In fact, I'll be a very interested spectator.'

'Edith——' Sasha began anxiously.

'Don't worry, Sasha. Listen, why don't you go and change?'

'What for?'

'Dinner! What else?'

'Oh. Do you think I ought to?'

'Yes, I do,' Edith said shortly. 'It will give you something to do while Heath and ... that woman are being private, instead of fiddling around in my kitchen.'

'That's a good idea,' Sasha said ingeniously. 'I'll do that. Just don't get too mad and break anything while I'm gone, Edith,' she added mischievously, and whisked herself out of the room as Edith turned on her menacingly.

But I don't really feel mischievous, she told herself as she emerged from a hasty shower. I feel so tense I could die! Take a deep breath, Sasha, she admonished herself, and calm down. You knew this was going to happen.

'I know,' she answered her reflection in the mirror, and was horrified to see two tears roll down her cheeks.

She sat down and reached for her hairbrush. But the soothing strokes of the brush couldn't eradicate the misery that was rising up in her throat, so she jumped up impatiently and searched through her wardrobe for something suitable to wear. She chose a pair of oatmeal suede culottes and a matching cashmere sweater and in a gesture of defiance, perhaps, spent some time putting up her hair. And her hand reached out automatically for the gold earrings Heath had given her, but she swallowed suddenly and changed her mind.

Then the rarely used dinner gong sounded, and she put her hands to her cheeks and stood like that for a moment before she forced herself to leave the room.

'It's going well,' Sasha whispered to Edith as she helped her clear the table. Heath and Veronica had taken their coffee into the lounge.

'Thanks to you,' said Edith. 'You're the life and soul of the party.'

'You make me sound like a clown!' Sasha retorted indignantly.

Edith softened as she cast a glance at Sasha's faintly flushed face and over-bright eyes. 'Not a clown,' she said, 'only a very sweet kid. Sasha? Oh no, it doesn't matter,' she added immediately. 'Go and have your coffee with them. Then you can retire gracefully if you want to.'

'And when will Brent be back?' Veronica asked Sasha.

Sasha shrugged and rolled her eyes. 'Heaven knows! They're in Papua New Guinea now, and according to his last letter everything that could go wrong, has. I suspect it will be a couple of months at least.'

She looked up to see Heath watching her and Veronica watching Heath.

Then Veronica looked at Sasha and said with an effort, 'I should have thought you'd be up there smoothing his path. I've heard a few little snippets of gossip about you two,' she went on with a teasing grin, 'and not only about your capabilities as a Girl Friday, which he found almost indispensable.'

Sasha blushed and could think of no reply. So she jumped up and said, 'Well, I guess you two have a lot to talk about. If you'll excuse me, I might leave you to it.'

Veronica leant back in her chair with an undisguised

look of relief on her face, but it was Heath's expression that startled Sasha just before she turned to go. There was so much enigmatic amusement in his eyes as they rested on her face that her heartbeat tripped and she found her mouth was dry and her pulses racing stupidly, and before she stopped to think, she found herself outside in the dark, stumbling along as if she was fleeing from something she couldn't name.

But finally when she tripped over a stone and grazed her knee, some sanity returned and she realised she was cold as well as acting stupidly, so she turned back and slowly retraced her steps.

She turned the corner of the house and almost ran slap bang into Veronica, who was striding across the gravel to her car with her keys in her hands. They both recoiled and then Sasha said in surprise, 'You're not going so soon, are you, Veronica?'

'Of course I am!' Veronica snapped at her.

'B-but why?' Sasha stammered, taken aback.

'You should know, you . . . bitch!' Veronica bit out. And then she laughed harshly at the look of bewilderment on Sasha's face. 'So naïve,' she marvelled. 'But while you might have fooled him, you don't fool me. And I'll tell you something else,' she said in a low voice as she put a hand on Sasha's arm and with surprising strength pulled her around to the other side of the car, away from the house, 'enjoy him while you've got him, *Blossom*, because you won't have him for long!'

Sasha stared into the other girl's furious eyes. 'I don't know what you're talking about,' she said quietly.

'Well then, I'll be more precise,' said Veronica, her voice gone cold with anger. 'You took advantage of him, didn't you, pet? You found him here sick and alone and rushed in as you've been dying to do for years! But if you think it's any more than gratitude he feels for you, perish the thought, Sasha. In fact if I were you, I'd back out now, because when he gets round to realising it, he's going to make your life hell. And I'll be on the sidelines cheering,' she added viciously.

Sasha blinked. 'I . . . I don't understand,' she whispered.

'Oh yes, you do!' Veronica snapped, and her next words were like a slap in the face. 'You set out to steal him from me as long ago as that night of the party. You grabbed the opportunity to turn what was really only a stupid little tiff into a solid wedge that night. You took it into your hot little hands and by some . . . freak choice of words managed to upstage me that night. But do you think I don't know why?' She stopped and took a hold of herself, then went on with a faint mocking smile. 'I must admit you showed a bit of initiative. I do give you that—you showed a bit more drive than the great herd of them, but really you're no different from the millions of women who watched him on television and drooled over him and all the dim little typists and shopgirls and bored housewives who dreamt stupid daydreams of snaring him and taming him . . . what a laugh!'

'But you're not laughing,' said Sasha before she could stop herself. 'I mean . . .'

And to her horror Veronica said scornfully, 'I know what you mean. And you'll know what *I* mean when Heath starts to get bored with you. Do you think I haven't seen him look at other women, toy with them? And do you think I don't know how cold and cruel he can be sometimes? But then I know the reverse side of it too. As no other woman has yet, or will. I know what it's like to be made love to by Heath as . . . as . . .' her voice dropped and thickened, 'as no other man can do it. I know what it's like to fight him and then give in to him and be taken to heights you wouldn't know existed! And I know what it's like to match my wits with his and see him look at me with that glint of admiration in his eyes you'll *never* see . . .

'And that's why I know,' she went on very slowly, her beautiful face contorted into an ugly mask of rage and hatred, 'he'll come back to me. So don't say I didn't warn you, Sasha,' she added spitefully, and then with an expression of disgust, dropped her hand from Sasha's arm and got into her car with an impatient toss of her head. She slammed the door and revved the motor and drove off with a spurt of gravel leaving Sasha standing there staring after her in a daze.

She was still staring at the disappearing tail lights when Heath came down the steps to stand beside her.

'Where were you? I was looking for you, Sasha.'

Then the roar of Veronica's engine, as she gunned it to leave the drive and hit the road, made Sasha flinch and caused Heath to look at her more closely and take in her pallor and the look of shock in her eyes.

He lifted his head and tightened his lips. 'What did she say to you?' he asked grimly as the sound of the car faded.

Sasha moistened her lips. 'I . . . I think she's gone mad,' she said weakly.

'Tell me,' he said quietly.

'I . . . no, it's nothing.' She started to shiver. 'I'm s-so cold.'

'Come inside,' he said unemotionally. 'What were you doing out here in the first place?'

'Well, I went for a walk,' she said dully as he escorted her up the front steps and into the warmth of the lounge.

'Without your coat?' He pushed her down into a chair beside the fire. 'You're half frozen. I know what you need. Stay there.'

She stayed with her hands stretched out towards the fire and in a few minutes he was back with two large Irish coffees.

Sasha sipped hers and grimaced slightly. 'It's very strong,' she said, not looking at him.

He shrugged. 'You were very cold. Now tell me what she said to you.'

Her lids lifted involuntarily to him. He was standing beside the fire with his hands shoved into his pockets and his coffee on the mantelpiece and there was an air of purpose about him that made her catch her breath. Think before you speak, Sasha, she tried to tell herself. But she found she couldn't even think let alone speak.

'Sasha!'

She made an effort. 'I suppose we don't like each other, that's all.'

'Neither of you showed it during the dinner,' he commented. 'Why don't you like each other?'

She said helplessly, 'You don't always need a reason. Some people just . . . antagonise each other.'

'Sasha,' he said on a dangerously quiet note, '*tell* me.'

'I don't want to!' she cried, suddenly close to tears. 'And you can't make me.'

'Yes, I can.' He leant forward and prised her coffee from her fingers and hauled her unceremoniously to her feet. 'Now start talking, dear, stubborn little stepsister,' he commanded softly. 'Otherwise I might be tempted to put you over my knee and spank you.'

She gasped. 'You *wouldn't*!' she blazed at him.

'Don't be too sure.' His fingers tightened about her wrists as she made a convulsive movement to free herself. 'Come on, Sasha,' he added curtly, 'don't be a child.'

'All *right*,' she snapped furiously, goaded by his words. 'I'll tell you! She thinks I'm trying to steal you away from her. She . . . she thinks I've tried to make you fall in love with me. Taken advantage of you, were her exact words. That's what she said to me. But if she only knew . . .' She stopped abruptly and her shoulders sagged.

'Knew what?' queried Heath, the deep blue fire of his eyes boring into her own.

'I was going to get in touch with her and ask her to come to you. In spite of . . . Edith, I was going to do it,' she said defiantly.

He let her wrist go suddenly that she sank back into the chair.

'Now why the hell would you have done that?' he asked coldly.

'Because she loves you, Heath. And you need her,' she whispered, looking up at him with her eyes wide and shining with unshed tears.

'Well, for once I agree with Edith,' he said flatly. 'But I just wish you'd stop discussing me behind my back and meddling in my affairs,' he added with a surge of savagery in his voice.

'I'm sorry,' she said hopelessly after a moment. Then, 'But I don't understand. Why should Veronica think those things? I thought . . . I mean, I tried to make it obvious I wanted you two to be alone—together. Why should she be so upset and so convinced I . . .'

'Oh, that,' he interrupted with a tinge of impatience, and half turned away from her. 'I told her that. At least, I told her you and I were getting engaged.'

His words caused the room to whirl so alarmingly before her eyes, she closed them experimentally. 'S-say that again?' she stammered.

He turned back to her and his lips twitched faintly.

'I told her we were getting engaged,' he said deliberately.

Sasha's eyes flew open. 'But,' she said incredulously, 'you . . . we . . . we can't! What about Brent?' She had no idea what made her say that, but then again, she often thought afterwards, wouldn't it have been what Heath expected her to say?

His eyes narrowed as he searched her face intently. Then he said coolly, 'What about him? You said yourself he'd probably be stuck in the highlands of New Guinea for months. And since you're all feeling so philanthropic towards me, he might not mind. After all, you got me into this, Sasha,' he added cruelly. 'If it hadn't been for you I'd have been thousands of miles away from Veronica, and the whole damn bunch of you, for that matter.'

A slow comprehension began to trickle into Sasha's mind.

'You didn't tell her, did you?' she said huskily. 'You don't want her to know.'

'I don't particularly want anyone to know,' Heath said irritably.

'But least of all her?'

He moved restlessly.

'. . . I see,' she said at last when he didn't answer.

'I doubt it,' he said wryly. 'But when you examine it, is it such a strange idea—us saying we're engaged? We're virtually living together like a sort of Darby and Joan couple as it is. And then when the thing's resolved, one way or another, we can put a stop to the charade.' He shrugged and cast himself down into the chair opposite.

'What . . . no,' Sasha said the last word hastily.

He looked at her derisively. 'What if I do go blind? Is that what you were going to say?' He studied her hot face thoughtfully. 'Sasha, from what the two specialists told me, in about a month's time they'll know whether the nerve is still healing or deteriorating. Now whichever way it goes, this bargain you forced me into ends then; and neither you nor anybody else will be dictating anything to me. Nor will they be stopping me from getting the hell out of here if I want to. Because if I need someone to hold my hand, I'd far rather pay someone to do it. Do you understand?'

'Why . . . why don't you give her a chance, at least?' she said tearfully.

'Because I know her better than you do, my dear,' he

said on an odd note. 'Some people could take it. She couldn't. It's better for her this way.'

Sasha stared into the fire. 'But I don't see why we should . . . deceive her like this.'

'I've just told you, I know her better than you do, Sasha. You're not the only stubborn woman in the world. This is the one way to keep her at bay.'

Sasha recalled some of the things Veronica had said to her and wondered. She said slowly, 'I don't know what to think.'

'It will only involve wearing a ring and playing a part for the benefit of any company we may get. I suspect now that Veronica knows I'm home, the whole of Sydney will know soon too. And it will only be for about a month.'

'Sometimes a month can be a very long time,' she said quietly.

Heath raised his eyebrows ironically. 'You're not wrong,' he said evenly but with an underlying note of strain, and she bit her lip as she realised just how long this month would be for him.

'If,' she cleared her throat, 'if you're very sure this is the way you want to do it?' she asked searchingly.

'Quite sure,' he said dryly.

'All . . . all right.'

He looked across at her anxious face from beneath half-closed lids and smiled suddenly. 'Good girl! Thank you. But you don't need to look as if you're going to the gallows.'

Sasha looked down at her hands and smiled herself. A curious little smile of self-mockery. Just for a moment there, you thought the impossible had happened, didn't you, Sasha? she told herself. When will you ever learn?

If Sasha had hoped to postpone having to explain this latest development to Edith, she found it was a forlorn hope because Heath did it for her over breakfast the next morning.

And he merely produced it as a fait accompli and watched interestedly as Edith turned a pale shade of purple and appeared to swell visibly before she jumped up and left the room with a smothered exclamation and slamming the door behind her.

Sasha sighed. 'I knew she wouldn't like it. But why didn't you try to explain it to her?'

'Why should I?' he said broodingly. 'She wouldn't believe a word of it anyway. She'd still be quite convinced it was a deep dark plot to ravish the girl she looks upon as the daughter she's never had.'

Sasha had to smile at that.

She found she wasn't smiling, though, when she herself tried to make the explanations to Edith.

'Oh, is that the line he spun you?' Edith said scornfully.

'But it's true, Edith!' said Sasha exasperatedly.

'Is it? Then tell me this. What about Mr Havelock? How are you going to explain it to him? Tell me that!'

Sasha sighed. She had never quite had the courage to explain about Brent to Edith and had hoped devoutly she would never be called upon to do it. Now there seemed to be no escape from it, and she couldn't deny it made strange telling. And when she had finished, she added despairingly and not quite truthfully, 'I only did it because I had to think up some reason for leaving my job!'

Edith stood staring at her with a rolling pin held aloft in her hand as if she'd forgotten she was holding it. Then she lowered it to the table and said carefully, 'Sasha, are you trying to tell me you've got yourself engaged to two men ... both times under false pretences?'

'I'm not actually engaged to Brent, Edith. And he knows all about it so ... but you mustn't ever tell Heath,' she said urgently.

Edith's lips twisted grimly. 'Oh, I won't,' she said. 'Believe me, I won't.' She was silent for a time. Then she turned from the pastry she was rolling with such ferocity. 'Just keep your wits about you,' she warned darkly, and refused to utter another word on the subject.

Doctor James chose that of all mornings to visit Heath and he was also told the news. But this time Sasha didn't attempt the tangled explanations Heath seemed so determined to omit, and weakly accepted the good doctor's delighted congratulations.

CHAPTER NINE

'YOU don't have to buy me a real ring, Heath,' Sasha said crossly as they stood in a plush, discreetly lit jeweller's store. 'She's not going to wrest it off me and examine it under a microscope—Veronica, I mean.'

'I know who you mean,' he replied imperturbably. 'But while I might not always be the spirit of gratitude personified, I do . . . appreciate what you've done for me.'

She closed her eyes briefly. 'If you think I want to be paid for it, think again,' she said shortly, and turned away from the tray of diamond rings.

'Sasha . . .'

'And don't "Sasha" me either!'

'Well, what?' he asked, his eyes gleaming with laughter. 'Blossom? Napoleon? Funny-face?'

'If you dare to call me any of those names,' she breathed, 'I'll run out of this shop screaming *rape* or something like that!'

'Er . . . this is a diamond of exceptional quality,' the formidably groomed middle-aged lady behind the counter said uncertainly as she cast Heath an odd glance. 'It's not large,' she went on, gaining confidence, 'but it's . . .'

'Not large!' Sasha interrupted scornfully. 'It's all of two carats. You could feed a family of ten on its worth for a year! Don't you have any of those synthetic diamonds I've read about?'

'Certainly not,' the saleslady said huffily. 'We only deal in genuine stones. I must say,' she added, 'most girls would be thrilled to bits with a ring like this.'

'I'm not most girls,' Sasha said coldly, and turned on her heel and strode out of the shop.

Heath caught her up in a few strides.

'I take it you're insulted, Sasha,' he said politely as he took hold of her arm and steered her into a milk bar. 'Is that why you behaved so badly?'

'*Yes.*'

He sat her down at a table and ordered two milk shakes.

'But you did agree to this engagement, didn't you?' he said as he came back to the table with the milk shakes.

'Yes,' she said through her teeth. And added conversationally, 'I must have been mad.'

'Why?' he asked with a faint grin that annoyed her intensely again.

She said fiercely, 'You asked me to wear a ring. All right, I don't so much mind wearing a ring. I just don't want to wear the most expensive ring in town because, although I consented, I still feel an awful fraud. And furthermore, for your information, I don't think engagement rings should be tokens of wealth. To me, that's like taking out an insurance policy. Something to hock when it all goes wrong.'

'You're right, you're not like most girls, Heath said wryly. 'But then I always knew that,' he added, and something in his eyes changed. 'Almost always,' he amended quietly. 'But tell me, if this was the real thing what kind of ring would you like?'

She set her teeth and then shrugged. 'If it was the real thing,' she looked away and her glance fell on an object on the table, 'this would do just as well.' She picked up the object, an aluminium ring top from a soft drink can, and pulled off the triangular tab before she slid it on to her finger. 'I mean, a ring is only the outward sign of a commitment, isn't it? It doesn't have any magical powers to make two people stay committed. That comes from within. Only problem is ... you'd have to find one that fits,' she murmured as she stared down at her hand and then lifted her head to smile ruefully at him. 'And I don't suppose it would fool Veronica,' she added with a little sigh.

'No,' he answered meditatively, staring down at her hand. 'But this might.' He lifted his head and reached into his pocket to withdraw a twist of paper that spilled on to the table a gold ring with a ruby, dark and mysteriously red, at its centre, and two baguette diamonds alongside.

Sasha caught her breath. 'That's ... your mother's,' she stammered.

'I know. Her engagement ring. I found it in the safe with a note that said she'd worn it right up until she'd married your father. She also said it was a ring only worn with great love and deep sorrow and that now it was rightfully mine from her ... and my father.'

'If you think I could wear that,' Sasha said shakily, 'well, it's worse than the diamond.'

'No, it's not, Sasha. It may not be the same kind of love you'd be wearing it with, but it's a kind of love all the same ...' Heath broke off and grimaced wryly. 'I didn't mean it to sound so corny, but it happens to be true, I think. Look, I know how hard it's been for you, how ... boorish I've been, and wallowing in self-pity too, but you've stuck it out through thick and thin. So you wouldn't be bringing anything false to this ring.'

She thought for a bit. 'Only to Veronica,' she said at last.

'If so, only for Veronica's own sake,' he said on a curiously detached note. Then he looked away and added idly, 'And you can give it back to me when it's all over.'

Sasha sighed again and sat back. 'I once before ruminated on this peculiar power you and your mother share,' she said resignedly. 'To bring a crazy logic to a thing—and I know it's crazy really. And also to make it almost impossible to refuse either of you anything.'

He lifted his eyebrows quizzically. 'Does that mean you'll wear it?'

'I suppose so.'

'With or without your own version of a ring?' he teased as he picked up his mother's ring.

'Oh! Without, I think.' She grinned and pulled the aluminium ring off her finger. 'But it might not fit either,' she said anxiously, and for a moment, in her heart of hearts, wished desperately that the ruby ring wouldn't. But Heath picked up her hand and slid it on to her finger experimentally. It fitted perfectly.

'Like the proverbial glove,' he said gravely, and released her hand.

She stared down at the ring on her finger and could think of nothing to say.

In some ways the month flew, despite her fears. And although Heath still refused to discuss his sight with her, certain little things seemed to indicate to her that the miracle she prayed for nightly might be occurring. Because less often did he seem curiously disorientated or cautious in his movements. And she longed to ask, but found she couldn't.

And as Heath had predicted, Veronica did do some checking up, although indirectly. They began to get other visitors—friends of Heath who were also friends of Veronica's, although some weren't.

George Smythe was one of those, not exactly a friend of Veronica's, and it was he who alerted Sasha to what was going on. He and Sasha were sitting on the verandah and Heath had gone in to pour them a pre-lunch drink.

'I think you're perfect for Heath, Sasha,' he said abruptly. 'Though some might not agree.'

'Oh?' was all she could manage to say.

'Yes. Veronica principally. In fact she's spreading some rather nasty rumours about you and Heath.'

'L-like what?' she stammered.

'That Heath is only marrying you out of gratitude because you've helped him through this bad patch.' He laughed suddenly. 'I must say,' he went on at last, 'for someone who claims she knows Heath as well as Veronica claims she does, I would have thought she knew him better than that.'

Sasha smiled uncomfortably.

'Unfortunately a few of their so-called friends have taken up the cause in a manner of speaking,' George went on.

'What do you mean?'

'Well, there's a fair amount of speculation going on, Sasha. The subject of you and Heath has become what they used to call on 'on-dit' round the traps. And I think a lot of people—no, let's be fair—some of those coming out to see Heath and welcome him home are also coming out to see for themselves the exact state of affairs between you two.'

'How could they?' Sasha burst out. 'How could she . . .' She stopped abruptly.

'My dear Sasha,' George replied equably, 'surely I don't have to remind you of that old saying—hell hath no fury like a woman scorned?'

'But . . .' Sasha stared at him horrified, 'it's not like that,' she said shakily.

'Oh, but it is, Sasha,' he said gently. 'I just thought I'd warn you,' he added softly as they heard Heath approaching.

George's revelations made life very hard for Sasha. Up until now, in front of other people, she and Heath had acted almost normally, like the good friends they sometimes were, although he put his arm around her more frequently than he was in the habit of doing, and held her hand. It had seemed quite natural, but following George's visit, Sasha couldn't help tensing whenever she heard a car drive up, which they seemed to do with alarming frequency, and she found it almost impossible to relax in company.

She thought Heath must have noticed this too, because he seemed more tense and less affable himself as the days went by.

That the strain was equally on him didn't occur to her until the fourth week of the vital month when he suddenly exploded after they had said goodbye to yet another visitor, this time an ex-colleague from his early journalist days.

'I can't stand much more of this,' he said tightly as they watched the car drive away. 'I haven't seen him for a good five years.'

Sasha bit her lip. 'It was your idea,' she said mildly.

'It was bloody not! Do you think I send out invitations?' he demanded furiously.

'I mean—for us to get engaged.'

'Well, I miscalculated,' he said coldly. 'I had no idea it would precipitate this kind of interest. The place is getting like Central Railway Station! Do you know why he came?' he asked with a gesture towards the driveway, 'because I happen to know his sister writes a society column in some magazine. Between the two of them, they'll probably hash up some story about us to titilate their readers. I'm only surprised he didn't ask if he could take some photos!'

The peculiar humour of the situation touched Sasha briefly. 'Perhaps because you weren't very nice to him?' she suggested with a grin.

But Heath wasn't amused. 'Anyway, he's the last,' he said moodily. 'I refuse to see another soul, and you may tell them what you like, Sasha. I don't give a damn.'

The unfairness of this struck her rather forcibly, and she opened her mouth to protest but shut it again as an idea came to her. She looked at him.

'Heath, we could go home,' she said tentatively.

'We *are* home,' he said after a moment with ill-concealed impatience as if he was wondering whether she'd lost her mind.

'No, I mean *my* home—across the fence. Edith gets someone in to keep it clean and aired, once a week. And nobody need know where we are. And it's only a few days to go now.'

Heath had been in the act of stalking inside, but he checked and swung back towards her. 'Are you serious?' he demanded.

'Of course. I'm not exactly enjoying ... all this, either.'

'What about Edith?'

'I think we should leave her here to fend off our visitors. Edith's very good at that kind of thing,' Sasha said with a smile.

A strange expression crossed his face—a blend of quizzical amusement and something deeper which she couldn't put her finger on.

She waited.

'Hmm,' he said at last. 'Truer words you never uttered. About Edith, I mean. Very well, if you want to, we'll go.'

Edith, however, didn't think it a good idea at all, for some strange reason, which apparently wasn't that she minded acting as a buffer between Heath and the public.

'Well then, why not?' Sasha said patiently.

'Because he can't hide from people for the rest of his life—if that's the way it's going to be. And how will you cope on your own?'

'Edith, there'll only be the two of us. Of course I can cope!'

'That's what I mean,' Edith said gloomily. 'But I don't suppose anything I can say will make you change your mind,' she added with an air of pious resignation that secretly made Sasha want to laugh.

Sasha discovered it was a strange experience sharing her home with Heath. It was much smaller than the Townsend house, but warm and very comfortable. And for the first few days the peace and quiet and change of surroundings seemed to soothe Heath. They played chess with her father's beautifully carved ivory chess set, read together, and because the weather had turned bitterly cold and windy in a last furious burst of winter, she exerted every fibre of her being into keeping him amused and occupied.

It never occurred to her how disastrously successful she was or how supremely thoughtless she had been in suggesting this retreat in the first place. Not until the fourth day of the fourth week, that was.

It was obvious Heath was in a strange, restless mood from the time he got up. He couldn't seem to settle to anything, and when Sasha asked if he would like to do the crossword with her, he told her abruptly he'd rather be left alone.

She noticed the dark circles beneath his eyes indicating a sleepless night, and thought she understood. So she stayed out of his way for most of the day, pottering around doing the domestic chores. Then she washed her hair later in the afternoon and sat in front of the fire to dry it and wonder about Heath, who had shrugged on his old sheepskin coat and gone out for a walk despite the weather.

She was still sitting in front of the fire when he came home just before dark—and caught her breath as he stopped in the lounge doorway, because he looked so well and vital and disturbingly big after his battle with the elements. So much like the old Heath.

But as he stood in the doorway watching her, there was nothing of the old Heath in his eyes that were nearly navy blue this afternoon. Only a strange animosity that made her shiver suddenly. Then he turned away abruptly and she didn't see him again until she set dinner on the table.

She had put on a loose ivory wool caftan with an amethyst border and taken special care with the meal and the table in a bid to coax him into a better mood.

A vain bid, however, she realised when he soon proved he wasn't in the mood for eating or talking, and finally, after a strained ten minutes or so, pushed his plate away with half his meal untouched. But her heart went out to him as she thought of the tension he must be going though, waiting and wondering what this next consultation would bring.

And she asked quietly, 'What is it, Heath?'

'Nothing.'

'Is there anything else you'd like?'

He didn't answer immediately. Then he said brusquely, 'Nothing you could give me, Sasha.'

She pushed her hair, which was floating in a shining cloud about her shoulders, back. 'You don't know that until you tell me, do you?' she said reasonably.

She stood up to clear the plates and was suddenly conscious of him watching her intently, so that her skin prickled faintly and her hands were't quite steady.

'All right, I will tell you, Sasha,' he said abruptly. 'I could do very well with the services of someone like yourself tonight. And the fact that your hair is gleaming and catching the light and I can smell the perfume of it and have to watch you in that very fetching garment that's so demure it's an invitation to rip it off in itself—all this isn't helping. But don't get me wrong, Sasha, it's not particularly you. You just happen to be on hand.'

She stood with her head bowed beneath the weight of his words and gasped as if he had plunged a knife into her heart.

Heath said tautly, 'You did want me to tell you, didn't you?'

She found she couldn't answer and she surreptitiously

wiped her tears away with the back of her hand and her head averted so that her hair hid her face.

'But I presume your concern for me stops short of that, Sasha,' he said mockingly. 'Or does it, I wonder ...'

'Stop it, Heath!' she said hoarsely, then suddenly made up her mind. 'I'm going.'

She turned away precipitously, but he was up in a flash, reaching for her, knocking over a chair and cursing viciously but managing to get her arm in an iron grip so that she cried out as he swung her towards him.

'You're not going anywhere, Sasha,' he ground out. 'You forced yourself on me, and the way things are I'd be a fool to knock you back.'

And then she was as angry as he was. 'I *hate* you!' she spat at him. 'And you were right ... oh, so right! You won't ever be ready to be tied down to one woman, because you're no better than a tom ... tomcat on the prowl! You have to equate every passable woman with sex. Well, I'm not interested, and what's more, I'm going—and you can't stop me. Goodbye, Heath,' she added with a flash of fury, and struggled desperately to free herself.

'Oh no, you don't, Sasha,' he replied, and pulled her into his arms.

'If you try to kiss me again, Heath,' she said very softly through her teeth, 'I'll bite you and scratch you with all my strength,' she threatened.

He stared down at her enigmatically and simply tightened his hold on her as she moved convulsively in his arms and finally subsided, panting.

'Has Brent ... slept with you, Sasha?' he asked then.

'That's got nothing to do with it!' she cried. 'Let me *go*, Heath!'

'But it has, technically speaking,' he drawled, not for a moment relaxing his hold. 'Yet something tells me he hasn't, and I can't help wondering why.'

'Well, it's none of your business in the first place,' she said fiercely. 'Not everyone is like you,' she added contemptuously. 'And anyway, I wouldn't be too sure, if I were you, because there's no way you can know and no way you're going to find out!'

Heath grinned then and all his old devilry glinted out of his deep blue eyes. 'Of course you're right,' he said lazily. 'About there being only one way to find out. All the same, I'd like to bet I'm right. Because you lack the cool someone with experience would show in handling these awkward little situations and immoral, dissolute persons—like myself, for instance.'

She tightened her lips, but he only laughed at the expression of outrage that filled her grey eyes and she knew she had no chance of outwitting him verbally. Her shoulders sagged involuntarily and she said wearily, 'Let me go, Heath.'

'In a minute. You know you'd enjoy it, Sasha—I'd make sure of that. We could do it on the rug in front of the fire if you liked. I'm sure you'd look like a lithe, supple goddess with the firelight playing on your pale, perfect skin and your beautiful hair . . .'

He loosened his arms a fraction as she stared up at him with her lips parted, and smiled faintly. 'Yes, you would,' he said, his voice suddenly curiously uneven. 'Your breasts and your thighs would glow like pale marble overlaid with gold . . . And I'd spend a long time just touching you, because that's half the pleasure of it. Skin touching skin, mine touching yours, first my hands, then my lips, then my body on yours and your hands on me . . .'

Sasha wanted to tear her eyes away from his, but found she couldn't, and she also found that she was breathing rapidly and her pulses were clamouring at the images he had created in her mind and a slow sort of heat was invading her body. And she marvelled at how he could do this to her. Then she thought of the one thing he hadn't said and she knew she'd hate herself, and perhaps him, if she submitted to the unbearable pleasure he was telling her of, knowing full well he didn't love her, and maybe was using her as a substitute.

And her bright head sank slowly and she shuddered.

'Sasha?' he said at last, very quietly and on quite a different note.

'No, Heath,' she said huskily. 'I can't—I'm sorry. It's . . . it's better if I go.'

'All right,' he said gently. 'I mean it's all right if you don't want me to make love to you. But you don't have to go.'

'Yes, I do,' she whispered. 'How can I *not*?'

He leant his head back against the wall and loosened his arms again so that they were just clasped loosely about her waist. 'Perhaps you could forgive me again,' he said at last. 'Please stay, Sasha. I don't know what I'd do without you and I don't know what moved me to . . . treat you like that. You see, even if you *were* my sister, I couldn't value you more.'

She closed her eyes, but the tears refused to be checked and he brought his fingers up to smudge them from her cheeks.

'Don't cry, Sasha,' he said, and pulled her forward so that her head was buried in his shoulder. 'I told you what kind of a man I was,' he said with a sort of suppressed violence, although he stroked her hair gently. 'Now you really know.'

I don't know what I know any more, she thought miserably. In fact I don't know *anything* any more outside of this moment . . .

'We could play Gilbert and Sullivan tonight,' he said, his voice deep while his hand still stroked her hair. 'Ever since I came home you haven't played any of it, and I know you have the whole range here. And do the crossword—and since we both didn't eat much we

could toast muffins on the fire and make some mulled
wine. Would you like that?'

She moved her head and swallowed her tears.

'Would you, Sasha?' He looked down at the head
cradled in his shoulder at last and closed his eyes
briefly. Then he took his hand from her hair and put his
fingers beneath her chin to tilt it upwards. 'Sasha?'

'I . . . yes.'

They did it all.

And gradually Sasha relaxed so that by the time they
went to bed it was as if nothing tempestuous had
happened between them—outwardly, at least.

But inwardly, as she climbed into the bed that had
been hers for as long as she could remember, the tears
were still there, and as she lay listening to the wind as
she had so many nights this winter, she knew finally
that she loved Heath Townsend because nothing he did
made her hate him—however hard she tried.

The next day the sun shone and a fragile, precarious
warmth in the air turned Sasha's thoughts to the
garden. So she went out armed with a pair of clippers
and started to prune the roses. Heath joined her after a
while and they worked together in a companionable
silence enjoying the first touch of spring.

And it was when he rolled up his sleeves that she
noticed the long, new-looking scratch on his forearm.

'When did you do that?' she asked. 'It looks as if
you've been having a go at the roses already.'

'Oh, that,' he said casually. 'I got my coat caught up
in an old barbed wire fence yesterday. I had to take it
off to get it disentangled and scratched myself in the
process. Which annoyed me somewhat, so that I took
an incautious step—it was down on the riverbank—and
I slipped and landed flat on my back.'

'Which annoyed you more?' she hazarded with a grin.

'Too right, as they say in the Antipodes.' He grinned back at her. 'Just as well there was no one around to hear!'

'Is that all the damage?' she asked.

'Almost. A few bruises, but I can't see them.'

'Ah,' she said understandingly, and they went back to pruning energetically.

That evening Sasha almost fell asleep in front of the fire. They were watching television and she was curled up in a big armchair like a cat.

'. . . Sasha.'

She yawned and rubbed her eyes.

'Yes?' she looked enquiringly at Heath.

'I said, isn't it time for bed?' he asked with a faint smile.

'Mmm,' she agreed sleepily. 'I'm so comfortable, though. Is this programme any good?'

'Not unless you like everything high-powered and bright and shiny new. The heroine looks as if she's stepped out of a store window display . . .'

It was a moment before it struck Sasha that his voice had sounded strange as he stopped speaking. She stirred and then sat up hurriedly as she saw him raise one hand to cover his left eye.

'What is it?' Her voice got caught in her throat.

He didn't answer.

'Heath?' She found her mouth had gone dry.

'I'm not . . . sure,' he said at last. 'This afternoon I though I had something in this eye. Now I feel as if I'm looking through a dust storm with strange . . . lights.'

Sasha jumped up with all thoughts of sleep fleeing from her mind. 'J-just stay there,' she said shakily. 'I'll call Doctor James . . .'

Events moved so swiftly after that, she had little time to draw breath. Doctor James refused to comment on the situation himself, but the speed with which he summoned an ambulance and the look of frustration in his eyes when he tried to contact the specialist and couldn't immediately, supported Sasha's own feeling that this was a very grave situation for Heath.

And when they finally got to town, to the private hospital he had booked Heath into, he left them at the reception desk and again went away to phone.

'Sasha?'

'Yes, Heath?'

'Don't stay. Go to the flat and get some sleep. You're exhausted as it is. The commissionaire knows you, he'll let you in.'

She looked down at him, on the stretcher as Doctor James had insisted, and opened her mouth to protest. But something in his pale, grim face stopped her.

'All right,' she said quietly, and pressed his hand gently. 'But I'll be back in the morning,' she warned, and forced herself to turn away as two orderlies came up to wheel him away.

But she didn't go. And it was Doctor James who discovered her in the waiting room. 'Sasha! I've been looking for you. Why aren't you with Heath?'

'He doesn't want me,' she said steadily. 'Is it . . . do you know anything yet?' Her voice cracked and he put an arm around her shoulders.

'I can't get hold of the right people at the moment, Sasha, and I'm no expert on ophthalmology or neurological problems, so I'd rather not say just yet. And as for Heath not wanting you with him when he's lying there imagining himself going blind and while I can't honestly give him any assurances to the contrary—my dear, I don't believe it,' he said gently, and took her hand. 'Come.'

The room Heath was in was dark apart from the light coming in from the window—reflected street lights from the city below—and it took a moment for Sasha's eyes to adjust to the gloom. Then she could make out his shape in the bed and the white bandage around his head.

He moved restlessly as if he sensed a presence and she said quickly, 'It's only me—Sasha,' and felt her heart beating in her throat as she waited for his reaction.

There was silence.

She licked her lips and said, 'I'm sorry. I sort of got hijacked into coming. I know you didn't want me to. I'll go . . .'

She turned away, but his voice reached her.

'How did you get hijacked, Sasha?'

'Well,' she temporised, then said wearily, 'I didn't ever go. And Doctor James found me. Goodnight, Heath . . .'

'Don't go, Sasha,' he said very quietly. 'Come here,' he added, and waited patiently as she approached the bed uncertainly. 'I'm glad you got hijacked, as you put it,' he said softly, and reached out a hand gropingly.

She put her hand into his and after a moment sat down on the edge of the bed. 'I won't stay long,' she said huskily.

'I wish to God you would.' He raised her hand to his mouth and kissed it. 'I don't have any designs on you, in case you're worried about that,' he said wryly, 'but I . . .'

He didn't finish, but she thought she heard him sigh as he released her hand and seemingly of their own accord, her fingers wandered to his head and felt his hair damp with sweat and the tension in his temples.

'I don't think they'd mind if I stayed for a while. If you wanted me to,' she whispered.

'Would you lie down beside me, Sasha?'

She didn't answer, only did as he bade quite naturally, on top of the covers. He slid one arm loosely around her waist and she stroked his hair.

And the gentle motion of her fingers seemed to open a floodgate.

'I thought I'd resigned myself to this, if it happened, Sasha. But it's the kind of thing you tell yourself, otherwise you'd go insane. And I've tried to console myself with the thought that I've seen it all—if it happens. That if people talk of yellow, say, I can picture a banana or a daffodil. Only it isn't much consolation, and I can't help wondering if I'll forget.' His voice was husky and very tired. 'But the worst thought of all is how I'm going to cope with being led around, fed . . . utterly dependent . . . I . . .' He stopped, and she felt the bitterness in him as if it was her own.

What can I say? she wondered. What can anyone say that doesn't sound trite and trivial? Wouldn't it be a jibe at his intelligence to say all the conventional things, because nothing is going to make it any easier for him.

And when she said nothing, just kept stroking his hair, he murmured at last, 'At least you understand, Sasha, don't you?'

'Yes, Heath,' she whispered.

He lifted his hand and she felt his fingers on her face, tracing the outline of her mouth. 'How come you understand these things so well?' he asked very quietly, his lips barely moving. 'No, don't try to answer,' he added with two fingers just lightly on her lips. Then his hand moved away to slide through her hair and he said on an oddly wry note, 'You once threatened to recite *The Man from Snowy River* to me. Would you think I was mad if I asked you to do it now?'

'Not mad,' she whispered, 'although you might think so once I get started. But you can always stop me. Let's see . . . There was movement on the station . . . for word had passed around, That the colt from old Regret, Had joined the wild bush horses—he was worth a thousand pound . . .'

It was his regular breathing that told her he was finally asleep, after she had gone through her whole repertoire of Banjo Patterson including *Clancy of the Overflow* and even *Weary Will the Wombat* which her mother had recited to her as a child.

And she just lay there for a long time drinking in his presence in the strange half-light and wondering at the magic Heath held for her whether he could see or not, and how defenceless he looked and how vulnerable, and how she had never thought to see Heath like this, at the very mercy of fate.

And every fibre of her being cried out in despair because she knew she was strong enough to see him through whatever might lie ahead, just as she knew he wouldn't let her, didn't really want her.

CHAPTER TEN

IT was a beautiful spring morning that greeted Sasha's weary eyes several hours later.

She hadn't left the hospital but had spent the time in the ward's waiting room while Heath slept. Which was the best thing for him, the Sister had told her, and added confidingly, 'I was going to give him something, but it's even better this way.'

Then there was a new Sister on duty and it was she who insisted Sasha go down to the cafeteria for some breakfast.

'Is he awake? Could I see him?' Sasha asked.

'Best not to at the moment, love. There's a team of specialists due to arrive any minute. But I'll tell the doctor where you are just in case. Now off you go before we have to find a bed for you too!' she added with firm kindness.

But when Sasha got back after ordering a breakfast she didn't eat and several cups of coffee, it seemed they were still with Heath, and her nerves already stretched to breaking point, seemed to stretch that little further.

Then Doctor James appeared and took one look at her and led her back to the cafeteria.

'Please just tell me,' she begged. 'I don't want to eat or drink!'

'Yes, you do,' he said briskly, and ordered two coffees. 'At least, I do. In fact I rather wish this was champagne!'

Sasha was glad she was sitting down. 'Is it . . . isn't it as bad . . .' she croaked, and wondered if her tired brain was playing tricks on her.

'No, Sasha,' he said compassionately as he took in

142

her white face. 'But it's an amazing coincidence, which was why, although I suspected it, I thought it best to be cautious. As I said, I'm no expert, and with Heath's history—but there, I'm rambling on. It appears these present symptoms Heath's suffering from are due to a detached retina which was probably caused by a fall he had a couple of days ago.'

Sasha stared at him. 'Yes,' she said wonderingly, 'he did fall, he told me about it. So it's nothing to do with the optic nerve?'

'No. It's a purely ophthalmic problem that can be corrected by an operation and a technique they call electro-coagulation which has a very reasonable success rate. And there's other news too. From what Heath's told them about his vision before this happened, and tests on his other eye, it would appear that the damage to or pressure on the optic nerve has healed itself. Over the last few weeks he's experienced none of the visual disabilities he had.'

'So . . . so even if this operation fails, he'll still have one good eye?' she said shakily.

'Yes. But I have high hopes of its success. He couldn't be in better hands.'

She let out a great sigh, 'Oh, thank you!' she said tearfully.

'Don't thank me, Sasha.' He smiled at her fondly. 'But I'm so pleased for you both.'

'When will this operation be?' she asked.

'They're preparing him now. Speed is the essence with this kind of thing. And afterwards he'll have to stay in bed with his eyes bandaged for a couple of days and it might take up to four or five weeks before he can resume a completely normal life. But of course he'll have you with him, won't he?' Doctor James added with a twinkle in his eye. 'What more could he want?' he said simply, and when Sasha coloured, he misread her embarrassment completely.

Sasha was still marvelling at this incredible piece of good fortune and feeling quite lightheaded with relief as she sat beside Heath after the operation.

The room was dim and quiet, and she sat beside the bed and rarely took her eyes off him. The dark gold of his hair lay across the bandage around his head and there was a faint blue shadow on his jaw as if he hadn't been very well shaved earlier, which she found unexpectedly touching.

And as she watched him breathing deeply and evenly, although she was dying to share the good news with him, in a sense she almost wished she could prolong this time.

I wonder why? she mused. Is it because I feel . . . sort of married to him like this? So close and as if he's in my care?

'I think it is,' she murmured aloud, and grimaced slightly.

Then Heath stirred and she leant forward and touched his fingers as they lay on the sheet.

His hand closed about hers and he relaxed and didn't move again.

The Sister slipped in and smiled warmly at her as she checked Heath's pulse. 'Shouldn't be long now,' she said kindly.

She was right. Not long afterwards, Heath stirred again and his hand suddenly clamped around hers.

'Sasha?' he said hoarsely. 'Is that you?'

'Yes.' She moistened her lips.

'Did I . . . dream it or . . .'

'No, it was no dream. It's going to be all right, Heath. But you'll have to have the bandage on for a while.'

A shudder of intense relief ran through his long frame and she felt tears on her cheeks. 'I'm so happy for you,' she said softly. 'So very happy for you.'

He said something she couldn't distinguish and then more distinctly, 'Don't go.'

'I won't,' she promised.

Four days later they were together again, although this time the bandage was off and Heath was sitting on his bed in the dimmed room listening to her as she read the paper.

'When do I get out of here?' he said suddenly, breaking in on her.

'When the doctors let you, I guess.'

'If you ask me they're being very cautious about it,' he said caustically and with so much of his old autocratic dynamism, Sasha had to smile.

But she said calmly, 'If you ask *me*, they're being very patient with you. Do you know what the Sister said to me this morning? She said, Miss Derwent, I don't know whether to envy you or pity you. All I know is, your fiancé is a right handful.' She looked at Heath quizzically. 'By the way, she doesn't like you chatting up her nurses.'

'I have not!' he protested laughingly. 'Is that what she said?'

Sasha wrinkled her nose and then relented. 'Not exactly,' she admitted. 'But she did say you've got them all in a bit of a flutter so that some of the younger ones—and the older ones—are getting about in a bit of a daze. I know how it can be,' she said with a tiny grin.

They laughed together. Then Heath said, 'I don't believe it, but just in case, isn't that all the more reason to get me out of here?'

'Oh no. When the doctor says yes and not a minute before.'

He muttered something half laughing beneath his breath. 'Sasha ...'

'Heath ...' They spoke together. 'You go first, Heath,' she said.

He eyed her. 'I was just going to tell you how pretty you look.'

Sasha glanced down at her outfit. A pale grey linen skirt with half pleats and matching grey suede shoes that she had teamed with a soft yellow blouse with long full sleeves and a cravat neck.

She shrugged. 'Thank you. It's new. To celebrate spring and . . . well, I just felt like celebrating.'

Heath leant back against the pillows still watching her. 'I like the way you've done your hair too.'

Her hair was lying loose today and she said with a grin, 'I haven't done anything to it!'

'I know. That's what I like about it.'

There was a small silence until she said, 'Heath? What we were talking about before? I mean, us . . . everyone thinking we're engaged. We don't have to keep that up now, do we?' she asked, staring down at the paper she had let flutter to the floor.

'Does it bother you?' he asked abruptly.

'No, it's not that.' She coloured faintly and then made herself look at him.

'What is it, then?'

'Well, I thought you might . . . you know,' she said helplessly.

'No.'

'Do you mean you don't know what I mean, or you don't . . . what do you mean?' she asked, suddenly exasperated by the look of mockery he sent her.

'That's what I was asking *you*,' he said politely. 'It seems we've got bogged down somewhere along the line.'

'We have not,' she said crossly. 'You know perfectly well what I mean. You're just . . . being difficult!'

A wicked blue glance shot her way. Then he looked downwards and said perfectly seriously, 'I enjoy a good fight with you, Sasha. I find it unusually stimulating. Go on.'

She gritted her teeth. 'Well, you're going to be disappointed today,' she said tightly, and got up to stand at the darkened window with her back to him.

He laughed softly at her.

'Don't do that!'

'I'm sorry,' he said, but unrepentantly. Then, 'Don't you think all these nice people,' he gestured widely, 'would get a bit of a shock if we suddenly became—disengaged?'

She shrugged. 'I guess they could live with it.' She fiddled with the cord of the blind.

His eyes narrowed at the tautness of her slim figure and he said softly but with a peculiarly grim undertone, 'That sounds strangely cynical coming from you, Sasha.'

'I might have had a good teacher.'

There was a strained silence. Then he said, 'Is Brent hovering on the horizon? Is that it?'

She swung round. 'No. That's not what I meant at all.'

'Then why the hurry?'

'There's no hurry on my part, Heath,' she said, speaking distinctly but with a gleam of anger darkening her eyes. 'I thought you might want an out.' But as she spoke she knew she wasn't telling the truth. There *was* an urgency on her part, something from within that told her that the longer she indulged in this masquerade, the harder it would be to put it behind her. In a sense it was like waiting for the axe to fall. Something that made her wonder how he would do it when he was ready. Something that told her that she wouldn't be so easily fobbed off as she had been the last time. Not to him, but to herself. She lifted her head which she had unconsciously lowered. 'After all, there's nothing to—no reason to keep pretending any more, is there?'

They stared at each other.

'So why are you crying, Sasha?' he asked at last.

'Am I? I didn't know I was.' She raised her wrists to her eyes. 'Maybe because I'm so happy for you.

Because you don't need me or anybody. You're free now. It's really something, isn't it?'

'Something to cry about?' he said sombrely. 'Nine times out of ten I would say no. But . . .'

'No, Heath,' she interrupted. 'Ten times out of ten. You've been *so* lucky.'

'Thanks to you.'

'No! It had nothing to do with me!'

'Blossom, it had a whole lot to do with you. That's why it's so hard to end.'

She moved forward and sat on the bed beside him. 'How can I explain?' she said gruffly.

Heath took her hands in his, 'You don't have to, Sasha.'

'Yes, I do. I . . .' She groped for words. 'I think you might be feeling very grateful. But really your gratitude should go to other people. And there's no reason now, not to open your heart to—to Veronica.'

There, it was out, she thought miserably. I've made myself say it.

She looked up at him obliquely from beneath her lashes and took an inward breath at the flash of—was it anger? she saw in his eyes. Then it was gone and he was saying equably, 'You're very determined to keep pushing me at Veronica, aren't you, Sasha? I thought you didn't like her.'

She smiled faintly. 'That's not the point is it?'

He considered for a moment with his fingers twisting his mother's engagement ring round and round Sasha's finger. Then his lips twitched, although he said gravely, 'As you once pointed out to me, we're a family whether we like it or not. So as to your prospective stepsister-in-law, you're entitled to a point of view at least.'

'Heath,' she said gently, 'when you do decide to marry I'm sure you wouldn't be so silly as to take into account what a stepsister would say. Least of all a stepsister.'

'Out of the mouths of babes,' he said at last, with a wry look.

'Not at all,' she said quietly. 'You gave me the same advice yourself once.'

Their eyes locked. Then Heath said meditatively, 'So I did. But I also gave you some very different advice once, if I recall.'

She shrugged slightly. 'I thought the second lot cancelled out the first,' she said with a grin.

'At the time it was intended to,' he murmured, and as she went to look away, lifted a hand to her chin and with gentle strength forced her to keep looking into his eyes. 'Why do I get the feeling, though, that you've disregarded my second lot of advice and are sticking to the first, Sasha?'

A trickle of apprehension ran through her as he gazed down at her more seriously and searchingly than ever before. Does he know? she wondered as that trickle became a tiny moment of panic and she lowered her eyelids in case he should see it, and at the same time willed herself to speak.

'Could it be circumstances?' she said at last, then went on to qualify what she'd said, trying to speak slowly and convincingly. 'I mean, I think circumstances might have made it look that way. But Brent did have to go away. And ...'

'And you decided you had to stay,' he filled in for her and abruptly released her chin. 'I see what you mean.' He looked down at her hand.

Oh no, you don't, Heath, she thought with an aching heart as she watched him, his lids with their gold-tipped lashes masking his eyes. But it's better this way. In fact it's the only way I can do it. I tried the other way once—it seems so long ago, and yet it seems like yesterday. But I could never do it again ...

His lids lifted unexpectedly and the deep blue fire of his eyes caught her off guard for an instant so that she felt flustered and wary and said hurriedly, 'But we're not talking about this, are we?'

'Aren't we?' he asked with his old look of mockery. 'No, you're right,' he added as she tried unsuccessfully to draw her hand away. 'We were talking about when would be a suitable time for us to terminate our engagement. When is Brent due home?'

She was taken aback slightly. 'I . . . I'm not sure. Not for another few weeks at least,' she stammered slightly. 'Why?'

'Because I thought if you could put up with me for another few weeks, say—until I get out of here and right back to normal, there seems no reason to rock the boat unnecessarily. After all,' he added with a gleam of humour, 'I'm supposed to take things quietly, aren't I? That's what everyone keeps telling me.' He pursed his lips in a very good imitation of Doctor James who had been in to see him daily, 'The main thing is not to get over-excited, Heath my lad! I'm not quite sure what he classes as over-excitement,' he went on in his normal tone, 'but I suspect what I have in mind wouldn't meet with his approval at all.' He looked at her significantly, testingly almost.

But Sasha had no doubt what he meant and her mind flew to Veronica and the two of them together again, and Veronica's words ran through her brain . . . I know what it's like to be made love to by Heath as no other man can do it . . . And to Sasha's mortification, she blushed vividly and wrenched her hand away and stood up. She heard Heath laugh softly as she crossed back to the window and for a moment, thought she hated him and would have given anything to tell him so. But she made an incredible effort and finally turned back to face him.

'All right,' she said evenly. 'But then we break it, whether you want to or not. And if you're still not ready for . . . for the excitement of Veronica, you'll just have to put up with Edith. In fact,' she added with a flash of irritability, 'Edith might even have a more soothing effect on you than I do. Could be just what the doctor ordered!'

She picked up her bag and made for the door, unwilling and unable to have any more words with Heath Townsend on this bright beautiful spring day that wasn't so bright and beautiful any more.

'Where are you going?'

'Out,' she flung over her shoulder. 'I'll be back tomorrow morning.'

She didn't see the strange look that crossed his face as she closed the door behind her. But she leant back against the door for a few minutes until her breathing steadied and her legs felt less like jelly and took the time to wonder why she was in such a state.

Two days later she was sitting on the side of the bed playing cards with him, the rhythm of their relationship since the night before the operation almost restored, although she wasn't quite sure how she'd managed it.

It had been so hard to come back yesterday, after stalking out the way she had. But beyond a certain look of speculation in his eyes when she had first entered the room, Heath had said nothing to make her feel uncomfortable, and gradually she had relaxed at the same time as she had realised rather bitterly that Heath could always make her relax if he set his mind to it. But she brushed aside the tiny spurt of resentment she felt, deliberately.

'Oh well,' she said lightly, coming back to the present and staring at the cards he'd laid down for her inspection on the wheeled table between them, 'that does it! You've not only won my life savings but all my worldly possessions. I can't believe how lucky you are at this game,' she added with some genuine exasperation as she looked back from his four aces to her full house.

'I really thought I had you then,' she went on confidingly.

'Luck's me middle name, lady,' Heath drawled lazily with an adopted American twang. 'Lucky in love, lucky at cards—you name it. I say,' he said, switching accents adroitly, 'there's one way you could pay off this debt, ma'am, but I hesitate to put it into words.'

She looked at him with a mortally wounded expression. 'Sir, I would rather spend the rest of my days in rags than succumb to your ungallant offer. I would rather die than accept such a fate! You are a cad, sir!' she added in ringing tones.

'You could always close your eyes and think of England,' he said insinuatingly.

'No, I couldn't, Heath,' she said with a giggle. 'Will you stop playing the fool? Or I'll leave you to play Patience on your own!' she threatened, but still laughing at his suddenly pious, hard-done-by expression.

'Dear, dear Sasha,' he pleaded, 'don't do that! Say you won't leave me!'

'Very well, I won't leave you. So long as you behave yourself.'

'I will,' he said fervently, and grabbed her hand to raise it to his lips, but a sudden movement from the doorway caused him to freeze and his navy blue eyes to open wide.

'What is it?' queried Sasha, and turned. And froze herself, momentarily, because standing in the doorway were the two people she had least expected to see there.

But there was no mistaking her father and Stephanie, and there was no mistaking the fact that Stephanie's eyes were riveted to Sasha's left hand, still curled around Heath's, and the ruby and diamond ring on her finger that was catching a stray gleam of light and reflecting it with a combination of mysterious red and white fire.

Stephanie was the first to break the silence.

She took an uncertain step forward and breathed, 'Heath? Sasha?' as her eyes travelled to each of their faces in turn. Then it was like a floodgate opened. 'Oh, my darlings!' she cried, 'I'm so happy for you both! I couldn't think of anything more perfect. You're just so right for each other. Oh, Sasha, if you only knew how happy this has made me,' she said huskily with tears streaming down her face as she reached the bed. 'My last dream come true . . .'

Sasha opened her mouth, but was immediately aware of the pressure of Heath's fingers on her own. Then her father was beside her and she saw how his face shone with happiness for her, and she swallowed hard, but the words refused to come and the moment was lost in a welter of affectionate embraces.

'But why didn't you tell us?' Stephanie asked. She glanced at Jonathan. 'This must have been what Edith meant when she warned us to expect a surprise,' she said helplessly and happily, and he put his arm round her affectionately and drew up a chair for her.

'Sit down, my love,' he said. 'I expect Edith thought they might want to tell us themselves.'

I suppose so,' said Stephanie, dabbing at her eyes with his handkerchief. 'Well, I must say you've quite taken the wind out of my sails,' she added ruefully, and sent Heath a mischievous look. 'I was all set to sweep in here and read you both the riot act. Yes,' she went on more in her usual manner, 'I'm not surprised you both look the picture of guilt and haven't got a word to say between you! If what Edith *did* tell me is correct and you didn't let me know—well, words fail me!' she said simply.

Heath spoke for the first time. 'I'm sorry. I thought this was the best way to do it—for you.' There was no mistaking the sincerity in his voice.

Stephanie dabbed at her eyes again. 'I appreciate

that, she said shakily after a moment, 'but ...' She
stopped and looked up at Jonathan sitting on the arm
of her chair and saw the faint warning in his eyes. 'Yes,
you're right. What's over is over. It is over?' she added
with a sudden anxious note in her voice as her eyes
roamed over Heath. 'I mean, you're not hiding
anything from me now, are you?'

Sasha found her voice suddenly. 'The operation was
entirely successful,' she said reassuringly. 'Heath's as
good as new—or almost,' she amended with a faint
quirk to her lips. 'In a couple of days his eyes will be
able to stand up to anything. But ...' She stopped.
She'd been going to say playfully—this engagement is
just a sham, don't take it seriously. Break it to them
lightly ...

'But what?' asked Stephanie with her brow furrowed.

'Well ...' Sasha licked her lips and knew somehow
that there was no way to break the news lightly without
perhaps breaking Stephanie's heart. Oh no, she
thought, that's ridiculous. But how?

It was Heath who unexpectedly took the matter out
of her hands. He said gently, 'I think what Sasha is
trying to tell you is that she wanted to let you know but
I wouldn't let her.'

'I was not!' she protested indignantly, and the words
were out before she stopped to think.

'Then what were you trying to say, my love?' he
queried with a smile lurking in his eyes. 'From our
respective parents' reaction, which was obviously quite
unpremeditated, I don't think you have to worry that
they'd object should we decide to get married
tomorrow.'

Sasha's lips formed a soundless O of astonishment
and the look she sent him was one of shock and
despair. But before it could become apparent to the two
other people in the room, he pulled her into his arms
and kissed her calmly on the lips.

'Heath!' she whispered faintly when at last his lips left hers. 'What are you doing?'

'I'm sorry,' he said to Stephanie and her father as he released her. 'As you can imagine, it's been rather a traumatic experience for us. And to top it off, Sasha was worried you might not approve.'

'Oh, Blossom!' Stephanie exclaimed with a sigh of relief.

But it was Sasha's father who unwittingly set the seal on Sasha's silence. 'Honey,' he said gently, 'if this is what you want I can only applaud your good taste and good sense. I have to admit that I long ago understood what you felt for Heath, just as I have to admit that I've always liked and admired you, Heath, man to man, and I have no doubt that you'll take good care of her. So you see, Sasha, this union has my blessing. Indeed, much more. Like Stephanie, it's fulfilled one of my greatest desires, and that's to see you happily married to the right man.'

CHAPTER ELEVEN

'WHY did you do it?'

Sasha's stunned words hung in the air.

Stephanie and Jonathan had just left them. They had only arrived in the country that morning and were understandably tired, and they had decided to spend the night at the flat. Sasha was to join them later for dinner.

Heath didn't answer immediately. Sasha was standing in her favourite spot by the window and her face was white and drained.

'Heath!' she said urgently.

He got up off the bed impatiently and came to stand beside her. 'It seemed like a good idea at the time,' he said abruptly.

She took a step away from him, her eyes wide with disbelief.

He looked at her assessingly, noting her pallor and the look of shock, and turned to look outside. 'Hell!' he muttered with unexpected savagery. 'They were so pleased. It would have been harder than taking candy from a kid.'

'I know, but we have to tell them some time,' she whispered.

There was a long silence during which her nerves seemed to stretch like piano wires.

But what he said finally came as an even greater shock. 'Perhaps we needn't tell them.' He turned back to her as she stood like a statue, 'After all, Sasha, maybe they're right. Maybe we are well suited. At least I know you're good for me . . .'

'What are you saying?' she cried, coming to life suddenly. 'What about Veronica?'

'Look, let's forget Veronica,' he said with his teeth gritted. 'I can assure you I have. It was an attraction that simply burnt itself out. It had to, and I'm not blaming her any more than I'm blaming myself, but it was far too volatile to last even if ... anyway, we'd have torn each other to pieces, Sasha. Do you think I didn't work that out months ago?'

'Then ... but ... why?' she said helplessly.

'Why what?'

'Why did we get engaged? I thought it was because you felt it was unfair to her if ... to expect her to spend her life with someone who was blind.'

'I didn't quite say that.'

'Yes, you *did*.'

'No, Sasha. All I said was I didn't think she could handle it. I meant—handle the fact that we really were finished, washed up, etc., gracefully. And I didn't feel like coping with it like some sitting duck at a fairground.' He shrugged. 'It was a rather devious way out, I guess. In more ways than one,' he added abruptly, and shoved his hands into his pockets.

'Heath, I wish you'd come out and told me straight,' Sasha said despairingly at last.

'What difference would it have made?' He watched her with narrowed eyes.

'I don't know,' she said feebly, at last. 'I can't think straight. Just ... well, why didn't you?'

He moved restlessly. 'It seemed like another good idea at the time. But this is beside the point, Sasha.'

'No,' she said swiftly. 'I mean, if you're sure about Veronica, you must wait until you find someone else.'

'I have found someone else,' he said carefully. 'Someone I know I can live with, someone I admire, someone I can trust. What more could you ask for?'

'Someone you love,' she said shakily. 'All those things you mentioned are fine, but without ... the right spark they could be nothing in a marriage. That's the difference between friendship and love. And friendship could turn into a noose around your neck, Heath, when you do find someone you love. So that, while I admire you too, I also have no intention of becoming that noose around your neck.'

'Maybe love will come, Sasha,' he said gently. And then added with an effort, 'Once, not so long ago, you would have been willing to try it.'

She coloured faintly and grimaced. 'I know. But I was very young and silly then. And as you predicted, I grew up.'

'Grew up to think I wouldn't be any good for you now, Sasha?'

She bit her lip and drew a deep breath. 'I'm trying to tell you it's not a good enough reason to marry a person because you think they might be good for you! Or because you're grateful to them. Or to please your mother!' she finished distraughtly.

His eyes smouldered and his lips tightened before he said coldly, 'You can acquit me on that count, Sasha. I'm not exactly proud of it, but I've never done anything just to please my mother.'

'I thought that's how this came up,' she said tightly.

'Well, you thought wrong. But tell me something. What about Brent? Why haven't you stopped this discussion by simply mentioning his name?'

Oh God! She thought. He's right. If I was in love with Brent it would have been the first thing I thought of . . .

'Tell me, Sasha,' he said instantly.

She licked her lips and for an insane moment she was tempted to tell him the truth, the whole truth, and take up his offer of marriage and make the best of it that she could. Then sanity prevailed and she knew that she would die slowly, within, like a withered tree, if she did. Because it would never be enough for her just to be 'good' for Heath. And it seemed to her that the best

way to put an end to this torture was to lie again. But it
was so *hard* . . .

'It's not easy to talk about Brent,' she heard herself
saying uncertainly. 'He's such a special person.' That
was true in one way. 'And,' she took a deep breath and
raised her eyes to his face, 'what I was really trying to
say to you was that I do understand, as I tried to tell
you the other day, how you feel. Gratitude and all that.
But the best way you could ever repay me for what was
really an enormous piece of impudence on my part
would be by taking your life up again and just being . . .
well, the old Heath. That was all I ever wanted,' she
said simply.

'I see,' he said at last in a curiously toneless voice.
Then, 'I hope you'll be very happy with him, Sasha.' He
turned away.

She closed her eyes and felt the tears trickle down her
cheeks. She rubbed her eyes desperately and then
reached for her purse for a hanky, only to find it taken
out of her hands.

'Here,' he said, and pressed a slip of cotton and lace
into her fingers.

'I don't know why I'm crying,' she said tremulously
when she had done the best she could with her face.
'I'm turning into one of those females who cry at the
drop of a hat!'

She looked up to see him staring at her sombrely and
felt as if her heart was being squeezed in her breast as
every detail of him seemed to burn itself into her
brain—the gold of his hair, the dark blue of his eyes,
the width of his shoulders . . . as if it was vital to record
it all in case she never saw him again.

She moved to ease the pain and said huskily, 'I'll
explain it to our respective parents tonight.' She bent
her head and slid the ruby ring from her finger. 'But I
must tell you, I do agree with them in one regard. As a
husband, you'd be something else again, Heath—for the

right wife.' She held out her hand to him with the ring lying in her palm. 'And you were right. I did wear it with a kind of love.'

He didn't move, just watched her, and there was a stillness about him that alarmed her faintly, so she looked around and set the ring on the bedside table, valiantly trying to control her shaking hand.

Then he spoke abruptly. 'When will the wedding be?'

'I don't know. Not ... not for a while. I ... might look for another job in the meantime. Just temporarily until B-Brent ties up this series.'

'Sasha . . .'

'I'm glad you called me that,' she interrupted with a tiny smile but still a gleam of tears in her eyes. 'If you'd called me Blossom or Napoleon or any of the other names I seem to attract, I'd have been most offended. I'm not Sasha Derwent for nothing,' she said, and smiled again at the faint frown that came to his eyes. 'My father used to say that to me,' she explained.

'Sasha Derwent—Sasha Havelock,' he murmured. 'Whichever, you're the only Sasha I've ever known or am likely to know.' He reached out a hand and touched her hair.

'I guess I could say the same for you, Heath Townsend,' she managed to whisper.

'So it's ... au revoir?'

'It's goodbye, Heath.'

'You're crying again,' he said softly.

'I told you . . .'

'Yes. I'm sorry I made such a ... rather, I'm sorry for all the times I made you cry.' He traced the path of her tears down one cheek.

She didn't know what to say, what to do. The emotion that clouded her throat made speech impossible, so she turned away and gathered up her purse blindly, then with a quick pressure of her fingers on his hand in passing, fled the room.

Nothing could have exceeded her expectations of the shock Stephanie and her father experienced when she told them that night, over dinner, that she and Heath weren't really engaged. It was like a visit to the dentist, she thought afterwards, when you'd consoled yourself that these things often turned out less fearful than you'd feared—only to find it was more painful than anything you'd experienced.

'I don't believe it!' Stephanie protested immediately.

Sasha looked appealingly at her father before she said quietly, 'I'm afraid it's true. We . . . I wanted to tell you this afternoon, but you were so thrilled. I don't know if it's ever happened to you when you know you should do something but just can't grasp the opportunity? That's what happened this afternoon.' As she spoke she was aware of her father watching her very closely.

'But I don't understand!' Stephanie said desperately. 'Why the pretence in the first place? Why the ring?'

Sasha explained as best she could.

'Well,' Stephanie said haltingly, 'I suppose I should be thankful he's not still infatuated with that woman, but . . .' She stopped speaking and rested her forehead desolately in the palm of her hand.

Nobody said anything for some time, but it was plain to see that Stephanie was grappling with her emotions, and even in the lamplit dining room, her face looked curiously old. So much older, Sasha thought.

'There's one thing that puzzles me,' her father said into the silence. 'I can appreciate how you found it difficult to explain in the light of our reactions, Sasha. In fact looking back I can now pinpoint the moment when you did try to explain. But I can't recall that Heath was under the same kind of strain. To me it seemed the opposite, if anything.'

He raised his grey eyes which Sasha had inherited to stare at her steadfastly and her heart missed a beat.

She lowered her eyes and decided the only thing she could do was to be truthful—to a degree. 'After you left, Heath did ask me to marry him.'

Stephanie whispered her name imploringly. '. . . Sasha!'

'I couldn't do it, Stephanie,' Sasha said very quietly. 'You see . . .'

'Is there someone else?'

Sasha flinched inwardly. Then she thought of all the complications she had invited as it was and decided quite suddenly that she could not launch into any more prevarications.

'That's not the point,' she said firmly. 'The point is I know why he did it. Out of a mixture of gratitude and perhaps because he's got to so used to having me around.'

'I see,' her father said at last, and Sasha had the uncomfortable feeling that her father saw a lot more than she had actually explained. But she was eternally grateful for the way he took command of things from then on.

He put his hand on Stephanie's as it lay slackly on the table and cast her a warning glance.

Stephanie opened her mouth to speak, but to Sasha's surprise, she closed it again and then with a touchingly affectionate gesture, laid her head on his shoulder for a moment.

'Well, my dear,' Jonathan Derwent said to Sasha, 'I think it's best if we forget about all this. Let's imagine we've only just arrived home and start off from there. You know, we've got nearly nine months to catch up on. And we've got cartloads of presents and mementoes and photos to show you.'

'What made you decide to come home like this out of the blue?' Sasha hastened to ask with a sigh of relief. 'You could have given us some warning!'

'A good solid bout of homesickness, my dear,' he told her. 'We were sitting in the umpteenth hotel room when it hit us jointly that there's no place like home!'

Sasha spent the week with her father and Stephanie at the flat. They had decided to stay in town until Heath was released from hospital and they visited him every day. But there seemed to be a tacit agreement between the three of them that Sasha didn't accompany them, and beyond progress reports, Heath wasn't discussed.

It seemed a silly situation, Sasha often thought, and she couldn't help wondering what the nursing staff and Doctor James would be thinking, but for the life of her she couldn't help but be grateful for it, even as she also wondered what had passed between Heath and his mother and her father on the subject.

The other problem that plagued her thoughts was what she was going to do with her life now. And it was her father again who came to the rescue.

He said easily one day over lunch, 'Much as we'd love to have you come back to the farm with us, Blossom, I suppose you're thinking of getting another job?'

'Yes,' she said ruefully. 'I mean—yes.'

'Anything in mind?'

'Not yet,' she confessed. 'I haven't really started looking.'

'Well, I bumped into an old friend of mine yesterday,' he said casually. 'He's a political journalist and he happened to mention that he was looking for a research assistant. I thought of you immediately because you have the political background and a research background.'

'It sounds like an ideal job for Sasha,' Stephanie said quietly. 'And I'd be delighted to give you a truthfully glowing reference.'

And that was how it happened.

Sasha got the job, although from something her employer let drop, she began to have doubts about the accuracy of her father's description of how they had 'bumped into' each other.

But for all that, she liked working for this older man with his gentle blue eyes that masked a fantastically sharp brain. And perhaps more to the point, he was very pleased with her work.

She had taken another flat in town, although she spent a lot of time commuting between Canberra and Sydney, attending parliamentary sessions. But her father and Stephanie made a point of pinning her down regularly for lunch or dinner in town and because it was second nature to Stephanie to discuss her only son, she couldn't help letting the odd items of news out, despite the peculiar restraint of the situation.

So that, two months after they had arrived home, Sasha knew that Heath was still at the farm with Stephanie and Jonathan living there too, and Edith also in residence; while her own home had been leased out. Privately she couldn't help wondering how long this arrangement would last and how Heath was occupying the time. But then she remembered that her father obviously had the knack of handling Stephanie, and maybe now Heath too.

But while she found she could discipline her thoughts about Heath most of the time, on other occasions, especially when she was spending a lonely evening in an impersonal hotel or on a late-night flight, he came back to haunt her with such startling clarity that she always caught her breath and had to fight back the tears.

It was the little things she sometimes thought she would never forget. His sometimes crazy sense of humour, the night she had lain in his arms and soothed him to sleep with poetry, how strong his arms had been when she had tried evade them . . .

And when she was very tired, the thought that haunted her most of all. Had it been only pride, stubborn unforgivable pride, that had stopped her from taking what he had offered?

She had written to Brent soon after she had started work again and had tried to explain how things had worked out; and in reply she had received two dozen red roses and a renewed offer of marriage from him. But with a let-out clause that had bothered her very much. For he had said, if the answer was still no, not to write, and if he didn't hear from her before he was due to leave New Guinea, he would proceed straight overseas where the final editing of the series would take place.

Sasha knew he had done it this way to save her embarrassment, but all the same she felt as if she was being let off too lightly. And she often pictured him in places like Madang and Kokoda and Port Moresby, and even went so far as to put pen to paper a couple of times only to think then—no, maybe his way is the best way.

So it came as a complete surprise nearly three months later one afternoon when she stepped out of the lift and fumbled in her bag for the key to her flat to look up and see the tall figure of Brent Havelock standing beside her doorway.

'Brent!' she exclaimed.

'Hello, Sasha.'

'Oh, Brent, it's so good to see you!'

'You too, Sasha.' He enveloped her in a bear-hug and then stood her at arm's length. 'You don't look well,' he said concernedly.

'I've been very busy lately,' she said with a grimace. 'But come inside and tell me all—no, let me put the kettle on first, then you must tell me everything. I'm dying to know!'

He told her over tea and a snack she had prepared.

'Of course, ratings are the one sure guide to the success or failure of something like this but the sponsors seem to be delighted with it,' he finished and grinned at her.

'I'm so glad,' she said simply. 'What will you do now?' she asked as she handed him a plate of sandwiches.

He took a cucumber sandwich and toyed with it for a while, not looking at her. Then he said abruptly, 'That rather depends on you, Sasha. I've come to renew my offer, you see.'

I should have known this was coming, she thought stupidly. I should have been prepared. What can I say?

Brent lifted his eyes suddenly and their glances locked for a small eternity before he said quietly, 'I see. Nothing's changed, has it?'

'I don't know,' she hoarsely at last.

'Yes, you do, Sasha,' he said gently. 'You're just as much in love with Heath as ever, aren't you?'

She moved restlessly. 'I don't know why. If I had any sense I wouldn't be.'

'Is it still Veronica?'

'No,' she said bleakly.

'He might just as well be blind,' he said roughly and with so much suppressed emotion that she blinked.

'But you said yourself, these are the things you can't change, Brent.'

'I said a lot of things,' he replied impatiently. 'What I didn't say was perhaps the most important. It's hell living without you, Sasha! But then I guess I don't have to explain that to you. No,' he added almost immediately, 'don't look so stricken.' He leant forward and took her face between his hands. 'I'll survive and so will you, my dear. Just remember that the offer's still open if ever you want it . . .'

And half an hour later he was gone.

But for days afterwards Sasha was still shaken by the

encounter and full of guilt and inwardly directed
mockery.

And then in the midst of all these recriminations—
Edith.

She was standing beside Sasha's front door just as
Brent had done, late one afternoon, and looking
particularly severe.

'Edith? Is something wrong?'

'Yes, Sasha,' Edith said gruffly, and bent forward to
kiss her on the cheek. 'You look pale, dear. Haven't
you been eating properly?'

'No—I mean yes. I mean, what is it? Dad?' Sasha
asked shakily.

'It's nothing like that,' Edith said briskly. 'Are you
going to invite me in?'

'Oh. Of course.' Sasha fumbled for her key and
unlocked the door. 'You gave me a fright,' she said as
she ushered Edith into the living room, took her hat
and coat and steered her to a chair. 'Would you like
something to drink?'

'Not yet, Sasha,' Edith said abruptly. 'I've got
something to tell you, and it won't be easy. Best off for
me just to say my piece. Sit down.'

This was so much like the old, authoritative Edith
that Sasha did as she was commanded with a faint grin.
'I'm ready.'

'It's Heath, Sasha. He's in love with you and has
been for a long time. And now he's eating his heart out
for you. As I suspect you might be for him,' added
Edith with a piercing look.

For a moment Sasha wondered if she was going mad,
had slipped into a world of fantasy. But there was
nothing dreamlike or even faintly unreal about the
uncompromising figure of Edith West sitting opposite
her, and she tried to speak, but no words would come.

'It's true, Sasha. And what's more, I've known it for
a long time.'

'But how?' Sasha asked weakly, at last.

'Well, in the first place, the one person he wanted to know about as soon as he got home was you. Where you were, what you were doing, how he could get in touch with you. And ... well, I showed him that article about you and Brent, and, God forgive me, Sasha, told him that I had high hopes of you two getting married.'

'You did that?' Sasha whispered.

'Yes, I did.' Edith looked strangely uncomfortable and for the first time her composure slipped a little. 'Sasha, I have to explain some things to you. I'm a crabby old spinster—I suppose that would be the best way to describe myself. And if there's anything more upsetting to someone like myself than someone like *Heath*—well, I can't think what it would be. He's rubbed me up the wrong way since I first laid eyes on him. It's a combination of a lot of things, I suppose, of seeing the way he treated women, seeing the way they reacted to him like a lot of blind, silly sheep,' she said contemptuously, then sighed suddenly. 'And if I'm honest, I suppose I have to admit, a sort of longing for my youth and perhaps another chance to take a different road.'

Sasha was struck speechless. Edith had not looked at her during her speech but concentrated on an imaginary loose thread in her skirt. Now she lifted her head and stared levelly across at Sasha.

'There's something else,' she said quietly. 'I knew you had . . .' She shrugged and looked suddenly awkward.

'Had a crush on Heath?' Sasha queried dryly. 'It seems everyone knew. I must have been very gauche.'

'No. Only very young,' Edith said gently. 'So you see,' she went on, 'when he came home and was so set on finding *you*, I thought to myself, oh no, Heath Townsend, she's got herself over you, found herself someone else perhaps, and I'm not going to let you start wreaking havoc with her heart again. And that's why I did what I did, Sasha.'

'Well, but . . .'

'But there's more,' Edith went on. 'The very same day I showed him the article was the day he saw the neuro-surgeon and found out that the operation he'd had might not have been successful.'

'You mean he didn't know until then?'

'No. But as soon as he found out, that's when he started to make plans to leave again. That's when I got onto Doctor James and begged him to find out exactly what the neuro-surgeon had said.'

Something clicked into place in Sasha's mind. 'I always wondered why he came home in the first place,' she said dazedly. 'I didn't know, but I thought . . . I remember thinking that surely he could have arranged his business from overseas.'

'Exactly,' Edith said sombrely. 'And perhaps you can imagine the dilemma I found myself in then. I knew I couldn't let him go, that Stephanie would never forgive me, but I also knew *I* couldn't keep him home. And in a sense that I'd been hoist with my own petard because you were probably the only person who could.'

'But look, I don't see . . .' Sasha began confusedly.

'Blossom, I didn't see for a while and then I refused to admit it, but the reason why he was so set on going again was because it was *your* life he didn't want to wreck—on two counts, because of what I'd told him about Brent Havelock, but even without that, because it was *you* he wouldn't inflict a blind man on.'

Sasha gazed at Edith helplessly. 'How can you be so sure?' she whispered.

Edith sighed. 'Because more and more clearly I could see the torture it was for him, living in the same house with you. I saw the way he looked at you when he didn't know I was watching. Why do you think I wasn't much surprised when he sent that Gardiner woman packing! Why do you think I was so wary when he suggested that false engagement and downright apprehensive when you took him off to your home? My dear, between us, we placed Heath in an impossible situation. And—well, I can only take my hat off to him for not . . . cracking. Which only makes me sure that he really cares about you, Sasha, as he's never cared for another woman.'

'But why didn't he tell me!' Sasha cried. 'He could have . . .'

'Could he?' Edith said wisely. 'Did you ever tell him about Mr Havelock? Did you ever explain that to him?'

Sasha stood up defensively and then moved across to the window.

'You didn't, did you, Sasha?'

'No.'

'Sasha, you and Heath are made for each other. Only a blind man or someone like myself wouldn't have realised that. Please. . . . think about it at least.'

Think about it, Sasha. Why can't I think about it? she wondered as she stared down at the busy street below. She leant her head against the pane of glass, but nothing came, other than a solid sense of disbelief.

'. . . Sasha?'

With a sigh she turned back to Edith. 'I will think about it,' she promised.

Edith stared at her searchingly. 'I can only ask you to forgive me too, dear,' she said gruffly.

'Oh, Edith!' Sasha went forward swiftly and knelt down beside the older woman's chair. 'What's to forgive?' she said gently.

'You're such a pet, Sasha,' said Edith, and sniffed. Then she added tentatively, 'He's gone away for a holiday. To the Barrier Reef.' She named an island and looked at Sasha expectantly.

'I'll . . . think about it,' said Sasha, unaware that

her voice lacked conviction so that Edith winced inwardly but came to a sudden decision not to labour her point.

Instead she said wryly, 'So much emotion! I could do with that drink now.'

CHAPTER TWELVE

IT was a poster in a travel agency's window that finally started Sasha thinking. She saw it the day after Edith's visit.

'Come to the beautiful Whitsunday Passage—Gateway to the Great Barrier Reef!' it said, and below were the almost lifesize figures of a man and a woman walking away into the sun, hand in hand on a smooth golden beach and with droplets of moisture still on their bodies.

Sasha hesitated, then turned back and walked into the agency and some time later came out clutching an air ticket and a hotel reservation slip in a small plastic folder—and a feeling of panic rising in her throat as well as a large hole in her cheque account.

'Suppose Edith is wrong?' she murmured as she made her way along the pavement crowded with lunch time shoppers. 'It's not impossible. In fact it's highly probable . . .'

It was the curious looks of several passers-by that reminded her it was a sign of madness to talk out loud to oneself, and she took a strong hold on herself.

But the passionate debate continued in her mind for the next few days as the weekend approached inexorably, and half a dozen times she reached for the telephone to cancel her flight. If Heath did feel as Edith claimed he did, why had he almost urged Brent to marry her without waiting? And why, once the threat of blindness had been removed, hadn't he at least told her then? Instead of asking her to marry him because she'd be good for him. . .? And on and on it went, until she felt sick and dizzy.

Then her employer took an unexpected hand. He looked at her thoughtfully on Friday afternoon and said she looked peaky, and seeing that Parliament wasn't sitting, why didn't she take the next week off and get herself a tan on some nice northern beach?

The coincidence of this seemed rather funny to her, because she could get a tan in Sydney too. But when she mentioned this he merely shrugged and said that a clean break from one's home town often did wonders for jaded bodies and minds, and he personally found nothing more relaxing than Queensland and the Barrier Reef, which he made a point of visiting every year.

Sasha had stared at him, momentarily transfixed, and found herself wondering if this was fate. A sign that she should go. Then she chided herself for being fanciful. Her fate was in her own hands, and if she did go, it would be because she herself had made the decision.

And she found that this was a strangely sustaining thought. Anyway, it sustained her sufficiently to climb aboard the aircraft on Saturday morning, but by the time she was halfway to Proserpine in Central Queensland, which was the jumping off point for the Whitsundays, she was again sick with fear and panic and quite certain that what she was doing would only re-open all the old wounds.

But by that time there was also a certain inevitability about it too, she found.

The plane touched down smoothly and she climbed out into the bright, warm humidity. There was a short wait and then she climbed into a helicopter and was whisked across a veritable paradise. Because as the tall cane fields of the mainland and the wooded, hilly coastline around Airlie Beach and Shute Harbour dropped away, a panorama of sparkling, placid waters studded with islands and coral atolls topped with dense green foliage and rimmed with white sands opened up below.

It was so beautiful Sasha caught her breath and for a while even forgot her problems as she drank it all in. And to top it off, the pilot spotted a whale in the blue of the water and circled around it.

Then they were coming down on one of the islands— the one on which according to Edith, Heath was staying—and all Sasha's doubts and misery came back to plague her.

The resort offered several different types of accommodation. Sasha had booked a room in the main building, but there were also self-contained bungalows scattered around the island that were far more private, and she thought that Heath would probably have chosen one of these, because his was still a familiar face.

But she couldn't be sure, and when she was finally in the privacy of her own room, she was struck by another thought which appalled her. Perhaps he wasn't alone? And she wondered distractedly why she hadn't thought of this earlier. Wasn't it bad enough that she'd heeded what were, after all, only Edith's suppositions without thinking of this possibility?

She sank down on to the bed and closed her eyes, conscious of one desire, and that was to escape. But of course it wasn't that simple to get off an island at a moment's notice.

'I'll just have to pretend it's a coincidence, my being here,' she murmured. 'That's all I can do!'

She sighed heavily and lay back on the bed. Outside, long shadows were creeping across the forecourt as the sun sank towards the horizon and for a time she just lay there, her mind numb and blank. Then, imperceptibly, she drifted off to sleep.

When she woke she didn't know where she was for a moment. It was pitch dark. She reached out a hand experimentally and found the shape of a lamp. She flicked it on, and immediately it all came back to her.

She glanced at her watch and with a wry grimace realised she had slept nearly twelve hours straight, fully clothed and curled up on the counterpane.

She stretched and then sat up and slid off the bed and crossed to the window. She could hear the murmur of the sea and the first faint twittering of birds which told her that dawn must be approaching, and she thought suddenly that this was the safest hour for her. Whatever else she did today, she could at least go down to the beach for a walk now and watch the sunrise, which was what her senses were clamouring for. She found she was in a fever to do it, so she changed hastily into her bikini, wrapped a colourful sarong about her, washed her face and brushed her hair and bunched it on top of her head, then slipped out of her room.

The building was very quiet and only dimly lit. And conveniently, the path over the dune and down to the beach was also discreetly lit at intervals. And as she came over the dune, she saw the first faint rim of light on the horizon.

It was an enchanting dawn that greeted her eyes as the darkness lessened and the bird chorus grew and the sea and the beach were washed with a living pink. It also gave her the feeling that she was the only person on the planet, and a cautious glance around seemed to confirm this. There was not another living soul in sight.

And the sea looked so inviting! Like a great lake with only small wavelets breaking on the sand because of the coral reef protection that made all these waterways so placid.

Her hands came up to the knot of her sarong at the same time as she knew she couldn't resist the temptation of the water, and she dropped it where she stood and ran down to the water's edge to wade in eagerly and then dive into its strangely warm, silky depths.

She wasn't sure how long she swam and floated, but -

eventually the sun itself was peeping over the horizon and she knew regretfully that it was time to come out.

There was still not a soul in sight as she walked up the beach to where she had dropped her sarong at the edge of the bushes—or to where she had thought she'd dropped it. But as she frowned and scratched her head and turned back towards the sea, a voice said behind her,

'Is this what you're looking for, Sasha?'

Her heart bumped frantically and her knees felt weak as she turned back in an awkward, stumbling fashion and found herself saying in a cracked, breathless voice and quite unassumed surprise, 'Heath?'

'Hello, Sasha,' he said quietly, and stepped forward to hand her the sarong.

He looked well, she thought fleetingly. In canvas shorts and an old T-shirt with his long legs brown and bare, there was nothing to distinguish this Heath from the person she had bathed with in Sydney so many months ago. Except perhaps that his eyes seemed to be a darker blue than ever.

'I . . . I didn't expect to see you,' she stammered, and added to herself, at least, not yet . . .

Something in his eyes changed. 'Nor I you,' he said after a moment. 'In fact I couldn't believe my eyes when the mermaid I perceived frolicking in the sea manifested itself as you, Sasha. How come you're here?'

'I'm on holiday,' she told him. 'I have a week off.' Coward, Sasha, she taunted herself. But she added ingenuously, 'How come *you're* here?'

'The same,' he said.

'Oh.' She looked down at herself and then at the sarong in her hand and rubbed herself down with it briefly before winding it around her. 'It's a nice place.'

'Have you been here long?'

'Only since yesterday. Are you . . . are you staying up at the hotel?'

He watched her as she took the band out of her hair and spread her fingers through it, then twisted it round her hand and wrung it out. 'No,' he said at last. 'I have a bungalow.'

There was an awkward pause. Awkward for Sasha at least as she tried to think of something to say. 'You're ... up very early,' she offered weakly at last.

He didn't agree or disagree, just studied her thoughtfully until she felt the colour steal into her cheeks and her heart begin to race because there was something frighteningly impersonal about his gaze.

Then he said casually, 'Would you care to join me for breakfast?'

'I ... well, yes, thank you,' she said helplessly.

And later in the day, when she was back in her own room, she found she was still frightened and disturbed. Only more so if anything.

She thought back to the hours she had spent with Heath after they had shared a breakfast of sweet, golden slices of paw-paw and bacon and eggs which he had cooked himself, surprisingly well. He'd shown her round the beautifully built wooden bungalow that blended into its tropical background and they'd swum together from his private beach which was really a little inlet between two rocky headlands.

It had all been very—ordinary, she thought. Just two people enjoying the sea and the sun. Except that it hadn't been ordinary at all, because those two people had been like strangers—polite, friendly strangers.

'It's as if everything that ever existed between us is dead now,' she murmured out loud as she dropped her sarong and bikini and stepped into the shower. 'The tolerance, the way we used to tease each other, the fact that despite everything, we *were* good friends, even the anger—it's all gone. He might be someone I've just met

and will only know for a week. Like two ships . . . Oh
dear! Edith *was* wrong, and I was wrong to come.'

And her despairing tears mingled with the shower
water as she wondered just how she was going to cope
with this week, but more particularly, the suggestion
Heath had made that they barbecue some steaks on the
beach that evening.

Several hours later she was still pondering the problem.
She had slept through the heat of the afternoon, but
through a crazy jumble of dreams which had featured
everyone she knew except Heath, although they had all
talked about him until she'd been only too happy to
wake up.

She also pondered briefly on what to wear and settled
on a more sophisticated version of the sarong she had
worn earlier because it seemed to fit in with the general
mood of the place. This one was a pale, clear yellow
with splashes of hibiscus colour on it, and she wore her
bikini beneath it and a pair of flat gold sandals.

She had left her hair loose and she studied the effect
in the mirror for a moment before turning away with a
dispirited shrug, and retreating from the room which
was beginning to remind her somewhat of a prison.

But although she had been in the frame of mind to
disregard her appearance, there were others who were
not, she discovered as she walked through the lounge,
which was an extension of the lobby. It was quite
crowded, but mainly with men enjoying a sundowner
while their wives and girl-friends put the finishing
touches to their toilettes.

And as Sasha walked through the area, unaware how
a day in the sun and the sea had caused her skin to look
peachy-golden, how her hair shone rich and auburn,
and how the sarong highlighted her figure as she
walked, a faint buzz of admiration grew, accompanied
by some faintly audible whistles and bold stares.

So that by the time she reached the main entrance and almost bumped into Heath coming up the front steps, she was flushed and embarrassed and poised for flight.

'What is it?' he asked immediately as he put out a hand to steady her.

'Nothing,' she said hastily, but added, 'Can we go? I didn't expect you to come and fetch me.'

He searched her hot face quizzically. 'You look as if someone's pinched your bottom, Sasha.'

'They wouldn't want to try,' she said crossly.

'I see,' he said with a tinge of irony, and took her hand in his as they descended the steps. 'Does the family know you're up here?' he added apparently inconsequently.

'No. I mean—why do you ask?' she enquired, sensing some kind of a trap.

'No reason,' he said idly as he steered her on to the pathway. 'It's just that this is a very sophisticated holiday resort. And not generally the kind girls of your sort choose for a holiday on their own. Unless . . .'

He let the word hang in the air tantalising.

'Unless what?' she asked resignedly.

'Unless they've come here to snare a wealthy husband,' Heath said with a grin.

Sasha stumbled slightly and his hand tightened on her own. But she said lightly, although with a curious blaze in her grey eyes, 'Oh. Oh well, I don't suppose that's true in my case, is it? After all, I've knocked back t . . . one of those already, haven't I?'

There was a strange silence and she refused to look at him as she wondered whether he'd noticed her slip. At the same time as she wondered why he hadn't mentioned Brent at all so far.

Then he said dryly, 'Touché, Blossom. Not that I really thought it of you. Nevertheless you might find that you've bitten off more than you can chew here.'

Secretly, she couldn't help wondering if he was right.

But she said casually, 'I can look after myself. I've had a bit of experience at it lately—I mean over the past year. I don't need a nursemaid,' she added with a touch of cynicism in her voice.

Heath stopped walking and swung her round to face him. 'So I noticed,' he murmured wryly with a movement of his head back towards the hotel. 'Back there you looked like a little girl who'd just had a nasty shock.'

'I . . . well, I wasn't expecting it, that's all,' she said wearily, and added, 'Look, Heath, I'm nearly twenty now!'

'Is that so?' he said easily. 'Nearly twenty? Why, sometimes it only seems like yesterday when you were telling me you were nearly nineteen. And all set on that occasion to embark on something . . . also foolhardy, if I recall.'

She stamped her foot and felt her face flood with hot colour again. 'I hate you, Heath Townsend!' she muttered through gritted teeth. 'And I hate the way you keep treating me like a child!'

Something glinted in his eyes then, something that warned her to run from him, but she stood her ground angrily. Until he said meditatively, 'If I treat you like a child in some ways perhaps it's because you *are* still a child in some ways. And perhaps that's why, whenever I've offered to treat you like a woman, you've—speaking metaphorically—run a mile?'

Sasha wrenched her hand out of his with a gasp and turned to flee up the path. But it was that bewitching hour between daylight and dusk and the lamps beside the path were competing feebly with the last rays of light and the dense ranks of foliage about them, so that she mistook a trailing creeper for a shadow and tripped, to sprawl headlong into the soft earth.

She groaned dismally. Not because she'd hurt herself but because almost immediately she could feel Heath's

hands on her, helping her up and then swinging her up
into his arms and wordlessly resisting all her struggles.

It wasn't far to the bungalow, and he kicked open the
door and strode through the living room to the
bedroom to deposit her none too gently on to the broad
double bed.

He flicked on the overhead light and then came back
to stand over her. 'Still running, Sasha?' he said coolly
as his eyes roamed over her, taking in her dirt-streaked
face and heaving breast.

Then he disappeared into the bathroom and returned
with a sponge and a towel and sat down beside her and
proceeded to wipe her hands and face quite impersonally
and as if she was a child of two.

Sasha suffered these ministrations mutinously; then
when he had finished she closed her eyes and brought
her hands up to cover her face. 'Please go away!' she
begged huskily.

She heard him laugh softly and felt his fingers on her
wrists and tensed, but with an easy strength and one
hand, he bore her own hands away from her face.

'Not until I've sorted something out, *Blossom*,' he
said, and she cringed, not only on account of that faint
emphasis but the air of menace his voice conveyed.

'What?' she whispered, and studied the ceiling rather
than look him in the eye.

'Why you're here. And don't give me the holiday bit,
because I don't buy it.'

She shrugged awkwardly. 'That's your problem,' she
said quietly, and thought miserably that only a few short
hours ago she'd been frightened by Heath's air of
distance from her. Now there was something equally
frightening about his proximity and not only physically.

'Then tell me about this second wealthy husband
you've spurned,' he said silkily, and grinned tightly as
her eyes flew back to his face. 'Yes, you were going to
say two, weren't you, Sasha? Which leaves me to

assume—by his absence as well and the lack of engagement rings or wedding bells—that you've given Brent his marching orders. Now I wonder why?'

'It's none of your business, Heath,' she said flatly.

'I'll decide that,' he said curtly. 'Are you up here to find a replacement for him, perhaps? Maybe I wasn't so far off the mark after all . . .'

With a superhuman effort she twisted beneath his hands and managed to scramble to her knees beside him but with her wrists still imprisoned in his hand.

'How *dare* you, Heath!' she breathed, her grey eyes sparking furiously and her face white with rage.

'Tell me, Sasha,' he said very quietly.

'I'd rather die than tell you anything,' she spat at him. 'Let . . . me *go*!' she panted.

'No.'

'Yes!' she cried. 'Or I'll . . . I'll . . .'

'Hit me?' he asked coolly, and smiled briefly.

Sasha closed her eyes in futile exasperation and took a deep breath to steady herself. 'Heath—you're hurting me,' she said stonily, because she would have rather died again than admit that just then.

'All right,' he said unexpectedly, and let her go.

She subsided on to her feet and rubbed her wrists resentfully as she eyed him warily.

'So you don't want to talk about Brent,' he said abruptly. 'You said that once before, didn't you? At least, that it was hard to talk about him because he was such a special person.' He looked at her narrowly. 'What made you change your mind?'

'I didn't. Not about that—he is a very special person.'

'But not good enough to marry? Then you led him a fine dance, didn't you, Sasha?' he said contemptuously.

She stared at him and something inside her seemed to shrivel as she thought of what he was accusing her of—

playing fast and loose with Brent. And she thought
bitterly of Edith's suppositions which had proved so
false and her own conviction of it which she had so
foolishly ignored.

And she said coldly, because suddenly she didn't care
what she said any more. 'You're a fine one to talk,
Heath! All this sentiment on Brent's behalf is very
touching, but it didn't stop you from asking me to
marry you . . . or . . . when you *knew* I was . . .' She said
the last words hurriedly and then stopped uncertainly,
already regretting her words and afraid again of
something in the deep blue of his eyes.

'What did I know?' he said very quietly. 'I'll tell you
what I knew, Sasha. That there was something not
quite right about your professed devotion for Brent.
Somehow it just didn't ring true, and it appears now
that I *was* right. What I can't work out is why you're
here. Particularly,' there was a curious emphasis on the
word that sent a trickle of added apprehension through
her, 'as it was your own father who urged me to come
here to this very island for a holiday to . . . put the final
touch to my convalescence, as he said.'

Sasha's eyes widened incredulously.

'Oh yes,' he said softly. 'So can you honestly tell me
you didn't know I was here, Sasha?'

She licked her lips and tried not to squirm beneath
his gaze at the same time as she mentally cursed her
father and Edith . . . and her employer, she thought
with a start. He must have been in on it too. But how
could they have put her in this intolerable position? On
the line like this, with her credibility in doubt and with
only one explanation that could redeem it. That old
explanation . . .

She closed her eyes and swallowed painfully. Say it,
Sasha, something from within urged her. But how can
I? she thought resentfully. Why should I make a fool of
myself again? So how are you going to get yourself out

of this then? that inner voice replied. More lies . . . lies
. . . lies!

The word seemed to pound in her head and she
dropped her head into her hands, only to raise it almost
immediately, and with her face white and set, she said
distinctly, 'Very well, I did know you were here. And I
came to tell you that I loved you and that it was no
delusion either. Because loving you seems to be a part
of me, like all my senses. It's as if,' she shrugged, 'as if I
wouldn't be Sasha Derwent if I didn't love you. But I'm
sure you don't really want to hear it . . .'

'Then why did you come to tell me?' Heath
interrupted swiftly, his voice low and harsh and his face
now almost as pale as hers.

She caught her breath. 'I . . . I don't know,' she
whispered, and felt her throat constrict. 'You'd have
thought I'd learnt my lesson, wouldn't you?' she added,
her eyes bright with tears. 'I wish I had, believe me,
because if it's an uncomfortable thought for you—for
me, it's like a thorn in my flesh I can't get rid of
however hard I try. But I will one day,' she vowed, and
moved her head defiantly. 'So don't think you have to
say anything or do anything!' she tossed at him, and her
eyes were defiant too, daring him to dispute this or
offer her any pity or platitudes.

Only he wasn't looking at her but staring across the
room with narrowed eyes and a curious tension visible
in the line of his shoulders. As if he was warding off a
blow of some kind. And when he spoke it was huskily
as if he was having difficulty with his voice. 'Tell me
about Brent, Sasha.'

Her shoulders sagged and the tears she had been
trying so desperately to keep at bay flowed down her
cheeks until he turned his head and said in a strangely
tortured way, 'Don't.'

She rubbed her eyes futilely. 'I can't help it. And I
didn't . . . lead Brent a fine dance, as you put it. At least

not intentionally *ever*. But that night, the first night at home after you came back, when you said what you did to me I . . . I . . .' She found it almost impossible to go on.

'You made it all up—about Brent?'

She nodded wordlessly.

'Why did he go along with you?'

'Because, he said, it was only what he'd wanted to do. I'd just . . . pre-empted him, sort of.' She shivered, and Heath noted it with a faint movement of his eyelids.

'So you decided to let it stand?'

'Only . . . because it seemed the best way—to deal with the situation. But he knew that because he knew, without me even having to tell him, how I felt about you.' A tiny frown knitted her forehead and she added desolately, 'I didn't mean to be so transparent and I'm sorry if I have been. Otherwise you might have been spared this embarrassment—again. It seems everyone knew and knows. But it will be different from now on.' She fiddled with the bedspread, not looking at him, then she raised her tear-streaked face and tried to smile.

Heath reached out a hand to push a gleaming strand of hair off her face, but there was no answering smile on his face as he said, 'Yes. It will be different from now on, Sasha. But not that way. Because as soon as I can arrange it, we'll be married, and then you won't ever have to worry again about who knows.'

She froze and her breath came in a great gasp that tore at her throat as she tried to speak. '. . . No! No, Heath. If I'd been prepared to marry you knowing you didn't love me, I'd have done it the first time you asked me!'

'Listen to me, Sasha,' he said, and captured her wrist as she tried to scramble off the bed.

'No!' she cried desperately. 'I've done with listening to . . . to everybody. If I hadn't listened I wouldn't be here now. Don't you understand?' she added wildly.

'Yes,' he said very quietly. 'And if you won't listen, I'll have to show you. Then *you* might understand.' And he pulled her into his arms and silenced her protests with his lips.

And when she finally lay dazed and still in his arms, he lifted his head and traced the outline of her throbbing mouth with one finger. 'You remind me of a flower, Sasha. A perfect blossom.' His arms tightened about her as she moved convulsively. 'God help me,' he went on his voice deep and uneven, 'I've been wanting to do this for so long, but now all I can think of is that I'll hurt you—as if I haven't hurt you enough already.'

She parted her lips to speak, but he shook his head almost imperceptibly. 'It's my turn now, Sasha. And when I've said it all, then if you want to, we can make love, and if you still love me and trust me, it will be the best way for you, and for me—as I told you once.'

His lips twisted with inward mockery as he studied her wide eyes. Then he said abruptly, 'Do you know when it first struck me what I'd turned my back on after my so noble renunciation of you, Sasha? Not more than two hours' flying time out of Melbourne. And it came like a loneliness that was so strong, I couldn't believe it. It was as if all the grace and beauty had gone out of the world for me and the rest was only . . . dust. And it grew, even although I repeated to myself over and over what I'd told you that . . . that night of the party. That you were too young to really know what you wanted and that I was too old, not so much in years, but in every other way, and that all I could bring to the sort of blinding purity that was Sasha Derwent was disillusionment and pain.'

His voice cracked slightly as he went on. 'And for almost two months I managed to convince myself of this. Then one day the urge to see you again was so strong, I couldn't resist it. And I tried to pretend to myself that it would be enough just to see you, but deep down I knew it wouldn't be. And I knew I'd been an incredible fool and that once I saw you again I'd do all in my power to rectify the mistake I made in letting you go the way I did. But on the very day I decided to get out of the living hell I was in . . .' He stopped and drew a deep breath. 'Well, I discovered there were some foolish mistakes you pay very dearly for. And . . . keep on paying for, it seemed, until I thought I'd go mad.'

Sasha stared up at him, almost afraid to breathe in case this was a dream that would shatter like a sheet of glass at the tiniest movement. But if anything, it was the dark, tortured look in his eyes perhaps more than his words that made her lift her hand and touch his face.

'Heath?' she breathed tremulously, her eyes huge and questioning.

He caught her hand and pressed it to his lips. Then he said indistinctly, 'I know. It must be hard to believe after some of the things I said and did. I even tried to convince myself that if I couldn't have you, at least I'd know you'd be safe with Brent. But I soon found out what poor consolation that thought was. You spoke . . . earlier of a thorn in your flesh—that was mine, one of them.' He closed his eyes and grimaced wryly. 'And when *I* said earlier that I knew there was something not quite right between you and Brent, I was never as confident of it as I made out. One day I'd be sure of it and the next, just as sure that it was only what I *wanted* to think. Then, that last day in the hospital, it seemed to me as if the time had come to put all my cards on the table. An entirely unexpected opportunity. But suddenly I couldn't do it. I just didn't have the courage.'

Sasha trembled in his arms, any doubts she might have still had about the unreality of what he was saying swept away by this confession of his own strange lack of self-confidence. For this was territory she knew well herself.

But Heath went on before she could speak. 'And for

these last few months I've regretted everything I said that day, but even more, what I didn't say. But the bitterest thought of all was that you'd taken my own advice—just as I'd told you you would, you'd grown out of me.'

She smiled faintly then, a wise little smile and he studied the curve of her lips intently with his lids half lowered.

'Sasha . . .'

'No, Heath,' she murmured. 'It's my turn again. Only it's not very original—just this. Could you kiss me, please?'

Never for a moment did she regret what followed. The way he kissed her or the way he laid her back on the bed and eased her out of her sarong and bikini with his hands lingering on her body and a bright steady flame in his eyes as he gazed down at her.

Then he lay down beside her and showed her what he had meant when he had said—that's half the pleasure of it. Skin touching skin, mine touching yours, first my hands, then my mouth, then my body on yours . . . And she couldn't believe the beauty of it, or Heath, or how he sensed her moment of panic when his movements became stronger and more urgent and how he retreated and murmured her name over and over again until she relaxed and such a tide of desire, evoked by his hands and his lips, rose within her that her transition from girlhood to womanhood was a thing of joy and splendour. And the tears she shed were only tears of supreme happiness.

'Don't cry,' said Heath, his lips just touching the corner of her mouth as they still lay within each other's arms.

'I'm not crying,' she whispered back. 'I mean, I am . . .'

'I know. You taste salty.'

'But only because I love you so, Heath. And I loved . . .' She broke off and coloured beneath his eyes.

'Loved me making love to you?' he supplied with a lurking smile.

'Yes,' she said huskily. 'Did you—I mean . . .' She stopped uncertainly.

He kissed her eyelids and when he spoke it wasn't quite evenly as he said, 'So much so, my darling, I'm afraid I'm hopelessly addicted to you. So you better take pity on me and marry me as soon as possible. But, Sasha . . .'

'Thank you for those kind words,' she interrupted teasingly. 'They make me feel like Topsy—growed and growed.'

'Sweetheart!'

'And I much prefer that to Blossom. Yes, Heath?' she queried demurely.

He raised himself on one elbow and grinned crookedly down at her. 'Never mind. I have just the solution for impudent child brides who won't let their elders get a word in edgeways. Come.'

He slid off the bed and swung her up into his arms.

'Where?' she asked in faint surprise as she linked her arms about his neck, and then gasped as he took no notice and stepped on to the terrace.

'Heath . . .'

'No one can see us,' he said reassuringly.

The night was dark but the light of a million stars cast a silver sheen on the water as he lowered her to her feet and held out his hand to her.

'You'll love this too.'

He was right. They waded in hand in hand and then he turned to her when they were about breast deep and took her in his arms, and Sasha caught her breath as the warm tropical sea caressed them, bringing a new dimension to the feel of his hard strong body against hers.

'Didn't I tell you?' he murmured, and kissed her throat. 'Now will you let me say what I wanted to say?'

She nodded wordlessly.

'I love you, Sasha. And without you . . . I'm nothing but a shell with no sense of direction, no purpose. And I might just as well be blind, because you're like the light of my life. Only there's no real reason for you to believe in me.'

'Yes, there is,' she said huskily. 'I always have, you see. But you've also convinced—perhaps the most doubting person in the world. And it was she who sent me to you.'

'I wouldn't call my mother that,' he said with a wry twist of his lips. 'And I thought it was your father who might have . . .' He stopped and looked at her curiously.

'It was neither of them,' she said. 'Although I suspect my father was a collaborator, because I don't think I ever fooled him—but it was Edith.'

Heath went very still. Then he said in dazed tones, 'Dear God!'

Sasha wound her arms around his neck. 'So you see, Heath,' she murmured, 'how could I not believe in you, when you come with such a high recommendation?'

'I . . . I'm amazed. And I can't think how I could ever repay her.'

'I can,' Sasha said quietly. 'We'll make her godmother to our first child.'

He kissed the tip of her nose. 'Then we definitely better get married soon,' he said with a laugh in his voice.

'You keep saying that,' she teased. 'I hope it doesn't mean you're going to make me wait until we're married before you . . . do what you did to me so beautifully just now.'

'Do you mean this?' he said innocently, and moulded her body to his intimately so that she closed her eyes at the wonder of it and buried her face in his shoulder in sudden shy confusion.

Until he tilted her head back with his hand in her hair and said huskily, 'My sweet Sasha.' His eyes roamed her face. 'I don't know what I've done to deserve you.'

'Nor I you, Heath,' she whispered.

'Then do I still have to wait for an invitation—or better still, may I reverse the procedure?'

'What do you mean?'

His eyes glinted. 'Can I say—kiss me, please, Sasha. Don't torment me like this?'

'Oh yes!'

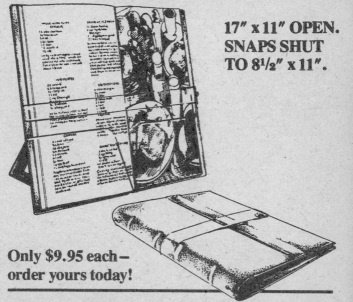